AND NEVER SAID A WORD

AND NEVER SAID A WORD

BY HEINRICH BÖLL

Translated
from the German by
LEILA VENNEWITZ

McGraw-Hill Book Company

NEW YORK   ST. LOUIS   SAN FRANCISCO
DÜSSELDORF   MEXICO   TORONTO

Book design by Kathy Peck.

234567890 BPBP 832

Library of Congress Cataloging in Publication Data

Böll, Heinrich, 1917–
And never said a word.
Translation of Und sagte kein einziges Wort.
I. Vennewitz, Leila.   II. Title.
PZ4.B6713Al   833′.9′14   77–18123
ISBN 0-07-006421-0

Paperback edition, 1979

Originally published in German under the title
Und sagte kein einziges Wort.
Copyright 1953 by Kiepenheuer & Witsch, Cologne, Germany.

TRANSLATOR'S ACKNOWLEDGMENT

To my husband, William—my gratitude for his share
in the work of this translation.

LEILA VENNEWITZ

1

After work I went around to the bank to cash my paycheck. There was a long line at the counter, and I waited half an hour, handed in my check, and saw the cashier pass it on to a girl in a yellow blouse. The girl turned to a file of account cards, found mine, handed the check back to the cashier, saying "O.K.," and the clean hands of the cashier counted out the bank notes onto the marble top. I counted them again, pushed my way toward the exit, and went to the little table beside the door to put the money in an envelope and write a note to my wife. On the table lay some pink deposit slips, and I took one and wrote on the back in pencil: "Must see you tomorrow, I'll phone before two." I put the note in the envelope, then tucked in the money, licked the gum on the flap of the envelope, hesitated, took out the money again, picked a ten-mark bill from the bundle, and put it in my coat pocket. I took my note out again, too, and added the words: "Kept 10 marks for myself. You'll get it back tomorrow. Kiss the children for me. Fred."

HEINRICH BÖLL

But now the envelope wouldn't stick, and I went over to the empty counter marked DEPOSITS. The girl behind the glass got up and raised the window. She was thin, with a dark complexion, and was wearing a pink sweater caught at the neck with an artificial rose. I asked her: "Could I have a piece of gummed tape, please?" She looked at me for a moment and hesitated, then tore a strip off a roll of brown gummed tape, handed it out to me without a word, and lowered the window again. I said "Thank you" to the pane of glass, went back to the table, stuck down the envelope, pulled on my beret, and left the bank.

It was raining when I came out, and in the street a few stray leaves were drifting down onto the asphalt. I stood in the entrance to the bank, waiting for the Number 12 to come around the corner, jumped on, and went as far as Tuckhoff Square. The streetcar was full of people, their clothes reeking of dampness. It was raining harder still when I jumped off at Tuckhoff Square, without having paid. I dashed under the awning of a snack stand, pushed my way to the counter, ordered a fried sausage and a cup of beef broth, asked for ten cigarettes, and changed the ten marks.

Taking a bite of sausage, I looked into the mirror that took up the entire rear wall of the booth. At first I didn't recognize myself, seeing that haggard face under the faded beret, and it suddenly came to me that I looked like one of the peddlers who used to come to my mother's door and were never turned away. The leaden despair in those faces pierced the dim light of our front hall when as a little boy I sometimes opened

2

the door to them. Then when my mother came—I had anxiously called her while keeping an eye on our coatrack—as soon as my mother came from the kitchen, drying her hands on her apron, a strange, reassuring glow would spread over the faces of those despairing figures who were trying to sell soap flakes or floor polish, razor blades or shoelaces. The happiness evoked on those gray faces by the mere sight of my mother had something terrible about it. My mother was a good woman. She could never turn anyone away from the door, she gave the beggars bread if we had any, money if we had any, offered them at least a cup of coffee, and, if we had nothing left in the house at all, she would give them some fresh water in a clean glass and the comfort of her eyes. All around our front-door bell was an accumulation of beggars' markings, of tramps' signs, and any peddler had a good chance of selling something as long as there was a single coin left in the house to pay for a pair of shoelaces. Nor did salesmen arouse my mother's suspicion, she could not resist the faces of those harried fellow sufferers either, and she would sign contracts, insurance policies, order forms; and I can remember how as a little boy lying in bed at night I would hear my father come home and the minute he entered the dining room the quarreling would start, an eerie quarreling in which my mother hardly spoke a word. She was a quiet woman. One of those men who used to turn up at our place wore a faded beret, like the one I'm wearing now, his name was Disch, he was an unfrocked priest, as I later discovered, and peddled soap flakes.

And now, as I was eating the sausage, which was hot enough to make my sore gums smart, I discovered in the flat mirror along the wall that I am beginning to look like that man Disch: my beret, my haggard face, and the despair in my eyes. But next to my face I saw in the mirror the faces of the other men at the counter, mouths opened wide to bite into sausages, I saw dark gaping gums behind yellow teeth with pink morsels of sausage meat falling into them, saw good hats, shabby ones, and the wet hair of hatless fellow customers, and the pink face of the waitress passing back and forth among them. With a cheerful smile she would fish hot sausages out of the pool of fat with a wooden fork, dab mustard on paper plates, pass back and forth among those eating mouths, collect dirty, mustard-daubed plates, hand out cigarettes and lemonade, take in money with those pink, rather stubby fingers, while the rain drummed on the awning.

In my face too, when I bit into the sausage, when my mouth opened to reveal the dark cavern of my throat behind yellowing teeth, I saw that expression of greed that shocked me in the faces of the others. Our heads were lined up like puppets in a Punch-and-Judy show, wreathed in the warm steam that rose from the frying pan. In my revulsion I pushed my way out again, hurrying through the rain into Mozart Street. Under store awnings people stood waiting, and on reaching Wagner's workshop I had once again to thrust my way through the crowd to the door, which I could barely pull open, and I was relieved when at last I walked down the steps and the smell of leather rose to meet me. There was a smell of the old sweat of old shoes, a smell of new leather, of cobbler's wax, and I could hear the hum of the old-fashioned stitching machine.

I walked past two women waiting on a bench, opened the glass door, and was glad to see my arrival bring a smile to Wagner's face. I have known him for thirty-five years. We used to live up in the air that is now over his shop, somewhere up there in the air above the cement roof of his workshop is where we used to live, and I remember taking my mother's slippers to him when I was only five. Now once again the crucifix hangs on the wall behind his stool, next to it the picture of Saint Crispin, a gentle old man with a gray beard, holding in his hands, which are not rough enough for a cobbler's, an iron trivet.

I shook hands with Wagner, and since he had nails in his mouth he merely nodded wordlessly toward the other stool. I sat down and pulled the envelope out of my pocket, and Wagner pushed his tobacco pouch and cigarette papers across the table. But my cigarette was still lit, I said "No thanks," held out the envelope toward him, and added: "Maybe. . . ."

He removed the nails from his mouth, rubbed his finger across his rough lips to make sure no little nail still clung there, and said: "Another little package for your wife—well, well."

He took the envelope and shook his head, saying: "I'll take care of it, I'll send my grandson across when he comes back from confession. In"—he glanced at the time—"in half an hour."

5

"She must have it today, there's money inside," I said. "I know," he said. I shook hands and left. As I climbed the steps again it occurred to me that I might have asked him for some money. I hesitated a moment, then walked up the last step and elbowed my way out through the people.

It was still raining when five minutes later I got off the bus at Benekam Street; I hurried along between the high-gabled façades of Gothic buildings that had been shored up to preserve them as historic monuments. Through the charred window frames I could see the heavy sky. Only one of those buildings is occupied; I stepped quickly under the porch roof, rang the bell, and waited.

In the maid's gentle brown eyes I could read that same pity I once used to feel for those types whom I am now obviously beginning to resemble. She took my coat and beret, shook them out by the door, and said: "My goodness, you must be wet through!" I nodded, went to the mirror, and ran my hands over my hair.

"Is Mrs. Beisem in?" I asked.

"No, she isn't."

"I wonder whether she's remembered that tomorrow's the first of the month?"

"No," said the maid. She showed me into the living room, moved the table closer to the tiled stove, and pulled up a chair, but I remained standing, leaning my back against the stove, and looked at the clock which for the last hundred and fifty years has been announcing the hour to the Beisem family. The room is crammed with antique furniture, and the windows contain the original Gothic leaded panes.

The maid brought me a cup of coffee, dragging Alfons behind her by his suspenders—the young Beisem whom I have undertaken to teach the rules of fractional arithmetic. The boy is robust, red-cheeked, and loves to play with horse chestnuts in the big garden— he collects them eagerly, gathering them up even from the adjacent buildings that are still vacant; and during the last few weeks I could see, when the window was open, long chains of chestnuts hanging out there between the trees.

I clasped my hands around the coffee cup, drinking down some of the warmth, and slowly repeated the rules of fractions to that healthy face, knowing that it was futile. He is a likable child, but stupid, stupid like his parents and his brothers and sisters; and there is only one intelligent person in the house: the maid.

Mr. Beisem deals in hides and scrap, is a likable fellow, and sometimes when I meet him and he chats with me for a few minutes I have the ridiculous feeling that he envies me my job. I have the impression that all his life he has suffered from the fact that more was expected of him than he could deliver: the management of a large business requiring as much toughness as intelligence. He lacks both, and when we meet he asks me about the details of my job with such passion that I am beginning to suspect that he would prefer to spend his entire life shut up in a small telephone exchange like me. He wants to know how I work the switchboard, how I put through long-distance calls, asks me about our professional jargon; and the idea that I can listen in on any conversation gives him a childish pleasure. "Interesting," he exclaims, over and over again, "how interesting!"

The hands of the clock moved slowly forward. I had the boy repeat the rules to me, dictated exercises, and sat smoking as I waited for them to be completed. It was quiet outside. Here in the heart of the city there was a silence like that of some tiny village in the steppes when the herds have moved away and only a few ailing old women have remained behind.

Fractions are divided by each other by multiplying them upside down. The child's eyes suddenly remained fixed on my face, and he said: "Clemens got a B in Latin."

I don't know whether he noticed how he had startled me. His remark suddenly dragged up my son's face, thrust it at me, the pale face of a thirteen-year-old, and I recalled that he sits beside Alfons.

"That's nice," I said with an effort, "how about you?"

"D," he said, and his eyes traveled doubtingly over my face, seemed to be looking for something, and I felt myself flush, yet at the same time was filled with indifference, for now they were all zeroing in on me, the faces of my wife, my children, gigantic faces, as if projected right into my own face, and I had to cover my eyes while I muttered: "Carry on, how do we multiply fractions with each other?" He repeated the rule in a low voice, looking at me all the while, but I didn't hear him: I saw my children harnessed to the deadly cycle that starts with hoisting a school satchel on your back and ends somewhere at an office desk. My mother used to watch me go off in the morning with my satchel on my back—and Käte, my wife, watches our children go off in the morning with their satchels on their backs.

I recited the rules of fractional arithmetic to this child's face, and some of them reemerged from this child's face back to me, and the hour passed, though slowly, and I had earned two marks fifty. I assigned the boy his homework for the next lesson, drank up the rest of the coffee, and went out into the hall. The maid had dried my coat and beret in the kitchen and gave me a smile as she helped me on with my coat. And as I stepped out onto the street I recalled the coarse, good-natured face of the girl, and I thought that I might have asked her for some money—I hesitated, only for an instant, turned up my coat collar as it was still raining, and hurried to the bus stop by the Church of the Seven Sorrows of Mary.

Ten minutes later I was sitting in a southern part of the city in a kitchen that smelled of vinegar, and a pale-faced girl with large, tawny eyes was reciting a list of Latin words. At one point the door to the next room opened and the thin face of a woman appeared in the door, a face with large, tawny eyes, and said: "Do make an effort, child, you know how hard it is for me to send you to school—and the lessons cost money."

The child made an effort, I made an effort, and the whole hour was spent in whispering lists of Latin words to each other, sentences and rules of syntax, and I knew that it was futile. And on the dot of ten minutes past three the thin woman came out of the next room trailing a pungent smell of vinegar, stroked the child's hair, looked at me, and asked: "Do you think she'll make it? The last test she got a C. Tomorrow they're going to have another."

I buttoned up my coat, pulled my wet beret out of my pocket, and said quietly: "She should make it." And I put my hand on the child's lackluster fair hair, and the woman said: "She's got to make it, she's all I have, my husband was killed in Vinitsa." I had a momentary vision of the dirty railway station at Vinitsa, full of rusty tractors—looked at the woman, and she suddenly plucked up her courage and said what she had been wanting to say all along: "Would you mind waiting for the money till...," and I agreed even before she had finished her sentence.

The little girl gave me a smile.

When I got outside the rain had stopped, the sun was shining, and a few large yellow leaves were drifting down from the trees onto the wet asphalt. I really wanted to go home to the Blocks', where I have been living for the last month, but I keep having the urge to do things, to assume burdens, when I know they won't lead to anything: I could have asked Wagner for money, could have asked the Beisems' maid or the woman who smelled of vinegar—I'm sure they would have given me something—but instead I walked to the streetcar stop, got on a Number 11, let myself be rocked about among wet passengers as far as Nacken-heim, aware that the hot sausage I had wolfed down at noon was beginning to nauseate me. In Nackenheim I walked between the neglected shrubs of a little park as far as Bückler's villa, rang the bell, and was shown into the living room by his girl friend. When I entered the room, Bückler tore off a strip of newspaper for a bookmark, snapped his book shut, and turned toward me with a stiff smile. He too has aged; he has been living for years now with this woman Dora, and their affair has become more boring than a marriage ever can. They watch each other with a remorselessness that has hardened their expressions, they call each other "Darling" and "Pussy," quarrel about money, are chained to each other.

On coming back into the room, Dora also tore a strip off the paper, placed it as a bookmark in her book, and poured me a cup of tea. On a table between them were some chocolates, a package of cigarettes, and a pot of tea.

"Nice to see you again," said Bückler. "Cigarette?"

"Yes, please," I said.

We smoked in silence. Dora sat with her face averted from me, and whenever I turned to look at her, her face wore a stony expression that immediately dis-solved into a smile when my eyes fell on her. Neither of them said a word, nor did I. I stubbed out my ciga-rette and suddenly said, into the midst of this silence:

"I could use some money. Maybe...."

But Bückler cut me short with a laugh, saying:

"Then you could use the same thing we've been needing all along, I'm glad to help you, but money, you know...."

I looked at Dora, and immediately her stony expression melted into a smile. She had sharp creases around her mouth, and she seemed to be inhaling the smoke of her cigarette more deeply than usual.

"I'm sorry," I said, "but you know how it is...."

"I know," he said, "no need to apologize, anyone can find himself in a jam."

"Well, I won't keep you," I said as I stood up.

"You're not keeping us at all," he said, and I could tell from the sudden animation in his voice that he meant it. Dora got up too, pushed me down by my shoulders, and in her eyes I could read the fear that I might leave. It struck me that they were genuinely pleased to see me. Dora offered me her cigarette case, poured me another cup of tea, and I sat down and tossed my beret onto a chair. But we remained silent, now and again exchanging a few words, and whenever I looked at Dora her stony face dissolved into a smile which, I had to assume, was sincere, for when I finally stood up and picked up my beret from the chair I realized that they were afraid of being alone with each other, that they were afraid of the books, the cigarettes, and the tea, that they dreaded the evening, the unending boredom they had taken upon themselves out of fear of the boredom of marriage.

Half an hour later I was standing in another part of town at the door of an old schoolmate's, pressing the bell. It was over a year since I had been to see him, and now when the curtain was drawn aside behind the tiny window in his front door I saw the dismay on his pasty, fleshy face. He opened the door, having meanwhile found time to put on a different face; and as we walked along the corridor steam came pouring out of a bathroom door and I could hear children squealing and his wife's shrill voice calling out: "Who is it?" I sat wtih him for half an hour in a room with greenish furniture smelling of mothballs, we talked of this and that, smoking, and when he began to reminisce about school his face lit up a bit, whereas I was seized with boredom, and with the smoke of my cigarette I puffed a question into his face:

"Can you lend me some money?"

He wasn't a bit surprised but started talking about the payments for the radio, the kitchen cabinets, the sofa, and about a winter coat for his wife. Then, changing the subject, he started talking about school again. I listened, and was seized by an uncanny feeling; he seemed to be talking about something that had happened two thousand years ago—I saw us in a dim past arguing with the janitor, throwing sponges against the blackboards, saw us having a smoke in the toilets as if they were the hovels of some prehistoric age. It was all so strange and remote that it frightened me, and I stood up saying: "I'm sorry . . . ," and turned to leave.

His expression became sullen again as we walked back along the corridor, and once again his wife's shrill voice called out something from the bathroom that I didn't catch, and he shouted back something sounding like "Cut it out, will you?" and the door closed behind me, and when I looked back from the dirty steps I could see that he had drawn back the curtain from the tiny window and was watching me leave.

I walked slowly back into town. It had started raining again, gently, there was a smell of decay and damp, and the gas lamps had already been lighted. In a tavern along the way I had a schnapps and watched a man standing at a jukebox who kept dropping in coins to listen to hit tunes. I blew the smoke of my cigarette across the counter, glanced into the solemn face of the landlady who looked to me like one of the damned, paid for my drink, and went on my way.

From the rubble heaps of bombed-out buildings the rain came running down onto the sidewalk in muddy rivulets, tinged with yellow or brown; and as I walked under the scaffoldings, chalky drops fell from them onto my coat.

I sat down in the Dominican Church and tried to pray. It was dark in the church, and little knots of men, women, and children were standing at the confessionals. Up at the altar two candles were burning, the red perpetual lamp was glowing as were the tiny lamps in the confessionals. Although I felt cold, I stayed almost an hour in the church. I heard the gentle murmurings in the confessionals, watched the people moving forward when someone emerged and walked into the central nave, covering his face with his hands. Once I saw the glowing red coils of an electric heater when a priest opened the door of the confessional and looked around to see how many people were still waiting. He seemed disappointed to see so many, almost a

dozen, and he went back into the confessional. I could
hear the heater being switched off and the gentle
murmurings starting again.

In my mind's eye I saw again the faces of all those I
had gone to see that afternoon, beginning with the girl
at the bank who had given me the piece of gummed
tape, the pink-faced woman at the snack stand, my own
face and gaping mouth with bits of sausage falling into
it, and the faded beret above my face; I saw Wagner's
face, the gentle, coarse face of the Beisems' maid, and
young Alfons Beisem, to whom I had whispered the
rules of fractional arithmetic, the girl in the kitchen
that smelled of vinegar, and I saw the station at Vinitsa,
dirty, full of rusty tractors, that station where her
father had been killed, saw her mother with the thin
face and large, tawny eyes, Bückler and that other
schoolmate, and the red face of the man who had been
standing at the jukebox in the tavern. I was getting
cold so I stood up, took some holy water from the
stoup at the entrance, crossed myself, and walked out
onto Böhnen Street; and when I entered Betzner's
tavern and sat down at the small table near the pinball
machine, I knew that all that afternoon, from the moment I had taken the ten-mark bill out of the envelope,
I had thought of nothing but Betzner's little tavern,
and I tossed my beret onto the peg, called across to the
counter: "A large schnapps, please," unbuttoned my
coat, and fumbled for a few coins in my jacket pocket.
I dropped a coin into the slot of the pinball machine,
pressed the button, releasing the little silver balls into
the runnel, used my right hand to pick up the schnapps

Betzner had brought me, propelled a ball onto the slanting board, and listened to the tune set off by the ball as it touched the contacts. And when I dug deeper into my pocket I found the five-mark piece I had almost forgotten: it had been lent me by the fellow who had relieved me at the switchboard.

I crouched over the machine, watching the bouncing of the little silver balls and listening to their tune, and I heard Betzner say under his breath to another man at the bar: "And there he'll stay till he's got rid of every last penny."

2

Again and again I count the money Fred has sent me: dark-green bank notes, light-green, blue ones, printed with the heads of peasant women crowned with wheatears, with buxom females symbolizing commerce or viticulture; hiding behind some hero's cloak, a man holding a wheel and probably meant to represent the crafts. Beside him an insipid maiden clasping the model of a bank to her bosom, at her feet a scroll and some architect's instruments. In the center of the green bank note, an unattractive hussy holding a pair of scales in her right hand and gazing past me out of her lifeless eyes. Ugly motifs frame these precious bank notes, the corners printed with numbers to represent their value. Oak leaves and wheatears, vine leaves and crossed hammers, are embossed on the coins, and on the reverse they carry the alarming symbol of the eagle with out-spread wings about to fly off in conquest.

The children watch me as I slip the bank notes through my hands, sorting them and piling up the coins: the monthly income of my husband, who is a switchboard operator at a diocesan office: three hundred and twenty marks and eighty-three pfennigs. I put aside one bank note for the rent, one for electricity and gas, one for health insurance, count out the money I owe the baker, and check over what's left: two hundred and forty marks. Fred has put in a note saying he has kept ten marks which he will return tomorrow. He will spend it on drink.

The children watch me; their faces are solemn and quiet, but I have a surprise for them: today they will be allowed to play in the corridor. The Frankes have left for the weekend to attend a conference of the Catholic League of Women. The Selbsteins, who live downstairs, will be away another two weeks on vacation; and as for the Hopfs, who have rented the room next to us, separated from us merely by a plaster wall —there's no need to ask the Hopfs. So the children will be allowed to play in the corridor, and that is a privilege that can't be underestimated.

"Is the money from Father?"

"Yes," I say.

"Is he still sick?"

"Yes—you can play in the corridor today, but don't break anything, and watch out for the wallpaper." And I savor my pleasure at seeing their faces light up as well as at being relieved of them when I start my Saturday chores.

The smell of preserving is still hanging about the corridor, although Mrs. Franke must have filled her three hundred jars by now. The smell of heated vinegar which in itself is enough to make Fred's bile flow, the smell of overcooked fruit and vegetables. The doors are locked, and the only thing left on the coatrack is the old hat Mr. Franke puts on when he goes down into the cellar. The new wallpaper comes as far as our door, and the new paint as far as the middle of the door panel forming the entrance to our apartment: a single room in which we have put up a plywood partition to make a cubicle where our baby sleeps and where we store some of our junk. The Frankes, on the other hand, have four rooms to themselves: kitchen, living room, bedroom, and an office where Mrs. Franke receives her numerous visitors. I don't know the number of committees, or the number of boards, I don't concern myself with her clubs. All I know is that the Church authorities have certified her urgent need for this room, a room that might not make us happy but would guarantee us the possibility of continuing a marriage.

At sixty, Mrs. Franke is still a beautiful woman; the strange brilliance of her eyes, however, with which she fascinates everybody, fills me with fear: those dark, hard eyes, her carefully groomed hair that is so skillfully dyed, her deep, slightly vibrating voice which only in speaking to me can suddenly become shrill, the cut of her clothes, the fact that every morning she receives Holy Communion, every month kisses the Bishop's ring when he receives the most prominent ladies of the diocese—these things make her a person it's futile to fight against. We know from experience, because we tried to fight her for six years and have now given up.

The children are playing in the corridor: they are so used to being quiet that now they don't even make noise when it is permitted. I can hardly hear them: they have tied empty cartons together to make a train that covers the entire length of the corridor and is now being carefully maneuvered back and forth. They set up stations, load empty cans and sticks, and I can be sure they will be occupied till suppertime. The baby is still asleep.

Once again I count the money, those precious, grubby bank notes whose cloying smell frightens me with its mildness, and I mentally add the ten marks Fred owes me. He will spend it on drink. He left us two months ago, spending the nights with friends or in some shelter or other, because he can no longer stand the cramped conditions of our apartment, the presence of Mrs. Franke, and those awful Hopfs next door. At the time we applied to the Housing Commission, which is building a development on the edge of town, they turned us down because Fred drinks and the priest gave me an unfavorable reference. He is annoyed that I don't take part in parish events. The chairman of the Housing Commission, however, is Mrs. Franke who, as a result of that decision, has managed to enhance her reputation as an irreproachable, selfless woman. For if she had granted us the new apartment, then our room, which she would like to have for a dining room, would have become available. So she turned us down to her own disadvantage.

As for me, ever since then I have been seized with a terror I hardly dare describe. Being the object of such hatred fills me with fear, and I shrink from partaking of the Body of Christ, the consumption of which seems to make Mrs. Franke more alarming every day. For the brilliance of her eyes is becoming harder and harder. And I am afraid to hear Holy Mass, even though the gentleness of the liturgy is one of my few remaining pleasures. I am afraid to see the priest at the altar, the same man whose voice I often hear in the office next door: the voice of a frustrated bon vivant who smokes good cigars and trades silly jokes with those club and committee women. They often laugh loudly next door, while I am required to ensure that the children don't make any noise because that might disturb the meeting. But I have long given up worrying about this, I let the children play and observe with dismay that they are no longer capable of being noisy. And sometimes while I am doing my shopping in the morning, when the baby is still asleep and the two oldest are in school, I slip into a church for a few moments, when there is no service on, and I sense the boundless peace emanating from the presence of God.

But sometimes Mrs. Franke displays tokens of feeling that frighten me even more than her hatred. At Christmas she came to invite us to join in a little celebration in her living room. And I saw us walking along the corridor as if into the depths of a mirror: Clemens and Carla first, then Fred, while I followed carrying the baby. We were walking into the depths of a mirror, and I saw us: we looked poor.

In the living room, which has remained unchanged for thirty years, I felt like a stranger, as if in another

21

world, a fish out of water: we have no business being among such furniture, among such paintings, we shouldn't sit down at tables covered with damask. And the Christmas-tree decorations salvaged by Mrs. Franke from before the war make my heart stop beating out of sheer terror: those glittering blue and gold baubles— that angel's hair and the dolls' faces of the glass angels, the Infant Jesus made of soap and lying in a rosewood crib, Mary and Joseph made of gaudily painted clay, beaming sweetly beneath the plaster-of-Paris scroll announcing "Peace to Mankind"—this furniture on which every week, for eight hours, the sweat of a cleaning woman is wasted, a woman who is paid fifty pfennigs an hour and is a member of the Mothers' Union, all this sterile cleanliness frightens me. Mr. Franke sat in a corner smoking his pipe. His bony frame is beginning to fill out, and I often hear his heavy tread as he comes up the stairs, his clumping footsteps, and his labored breathing goes past my room into the depths of the corridor.

The children are afraid of such furniture, which they don't see very often. They sit down hesitantly on the leather upholstery, so shy and silent that I could have wept. Plates of goodies had been prepared for each of them, and there were presents: socks, and the mandatory clay piggy bank that has been a feature of Christmas in the Franke family for the last thirty-five years.

Fred was scowling, and I could tell that he regretted having accepted the invitation; he stood leaning against the windowsill, pulled a loose cigarette from his pocket, slowly smoothed it, then lit it.

Mrs. Franke filled the glasses with wine and pushed bright china mugs of lemonade toward the children. The mugs are painted with scenes from the fairy tale about the wolf and the seven little goats.

We drank. Fred emptied his glass at one draft, held it speculatively in one hand, apparently contemplating the taste of the wine. At moments like that I admire him, for his face revealed that which needed no words to express. Two piggy banks and a glass of wine, five minutes of sentimentality, cannot disguise the fact that our apartment is too small.

This ghastly visit ended with cool good-byes, and I could read in Mrs. Franke's eyes everything she would be telling her friends about it: to the innumerable curses under which we labor is now added that of obvious ingratitude and rudeness, and for herself two more tiers on the many-tiered crown of martyrdom.

Mr. Franke rarely says anything, but when he knows his wife is out he sometimes sticks his head around our door and, without a word, lays a bar of chocolate on the table just inside, and sometimes I find a bank note hidden under the wrapper, and sometimes I can hear him talking to the children in the corridor. He stops them, mumbles a few words, and the children tell me he strokes their heads and says "nice things" to them.

But Mrs. Franke is not like that, she is garrulous and lively, devoid of tenderness. She comes from an old merchant family in the city which has been changing the commodities of their trade from generation to generation, advancing to ever more precious ones: from oil, salt, and flour, from fish and cloth, they progressed to wine, then they went into politics, sinking from there to real estate, and nowadays I sometimes think they are trading in the most precious commodity of all: God.

Only on rare occasions does Mrs. Franke show any tenderness: primarily when she speaks of money. She says the word with a tenderness that frightens me, the way some people utter the words Life, Love, Death, or God, gently, with a tinge of awe in their voices. The brilliance of her eyes dims a little, and her features become younger when she speaks of gold and of her jars of preserves, both being treasures she won't allow to be violated. Fear grips me sometimes when I am in the cellar to fetch coal or potatoes, and I happen to hear her counting the jars down there: in a low, soft voice, murmuring, chanting the numbers like the cadences of a secret liturgy, and her voice reminds me of the voice of a nun at prayer—and often I abandon my pail, fleeing upstairs to hold my children close, sensing that I have to protect them from something. And the children stare at me, the eyes of my son, who is beginning to grow up, and the gentle dark eyes of my daughter, they stare at me, understanding and not understanding—and they hesitate as they join me in the prayers I begin to recite, the intoxicating monotone of a litany or the phrases of the Paternoster that fall awkwardly from our lips.

But by now it is three o'clock, and all of a sudden the fear of Sunday erupts outside, noise bursts into the back courtyard, I can hear voices announcing a gay Saturday afternoon, and my heart begins to freeze over in my body. Once again I count out the money, look at the deadly dull pictures on the bank notes, and finally make up my mind to start spending it. Out in the corridor the children are laughing, the baby has woken up, and I must get going on my chores, and as I raise my eyes from the table I had been leaning on as my thoughts roamed, my gaze falls on the walls of our room that are hung with cheap prints: with the over-sweet faces of Renoir's women—they seem like strangers to me, so strange that I cannot understand how I could endure them a bare half hour ago. I take them down, tear them in half with steady hands, and throw the pieces into the garbage pail that I must shortly carry downstairs. My gaze travels along our walls, nothing finds mercy in my eyes except the crucifix over the door and a drawing by an artist, unknown to me, whose maze of lines and sparse colors had never meant any-thing to me but which I suddenly find I can grasp without understanding them.

3

Dawn was beginning to break as I left the station, and the streets were still empty. They ran diagonally past a block of buildings whose fronts had been repaired with unsightly patches of plaster. It was cold, and a few taxi drivers were standing around shivering in the station square, their hands buried deep in their overcoat pockets, and for a moment those four or five pallid faces under their blue peaked caps turned toward me; they moved as one, like puppets on a string. Only a moment, then the faces snapped back into their old position, turned toward the station exit.

There were not even prostitutes on the streets at this hour, and as I turned slowly around I saw the big hand of the station clock creep onto the nine: it was a quarter to six. I turned into the street leading to the right past the building, and looked carefully into the store windows: somewhere a café or a tavern was bound to be open, or one of those stalls which, although I detest them, I prefer to waiting rooms, whose coffee at this time of the day is tepid and whose insipid, warmed-up beef broth tastes of barracks. I turned up my coat collar, carefully folding the corners over each other, and brushed the loose black dirt from my trousers and overcoat.

The night before, I had drunk more than usual, and toward one in the morning I had gone into the station to see Max, who sometimes gives me a place to bed down. Max works at the baggage check—I met him during the war—and in the middle of the checkroom there is a big radiator encased in a wooden frame with a bench attached. Here all those who work on the station's lower level come for a break: porters, baggage-room attendants, and elevator operators. The wooden frame leaves enough room for me to crawl behind it, and on the floor there is a wider space where it is dark and warm, and I feel at peace as I lie there, my heart is at rest, and the alcohol courses through my veins; the muffled roar of trains entering and leaving the station, the thudding of the baggage carts overhead, the hum of the elevators—sounds that in the darkness seem darker still to me—soon lull me to sleep. Sometimes, too, I weep down there, when I think of Käte and the kids, I weep, knowing that the tears of an alcoholic don't count, carry no weight—and I am aware of something that I would call not pangs of conscience, just pangs. I used to drink even before the war, but people seem to have forgotten that, and my low moral status is regarded with a certain tolerance because they can say of me: He fought in the war.

I cleaned myself up as carefully as I could, looking into the mirror at the rear of a café window, and the mirror reflected my sparse figure over and over again into infinity like an imaginary bowling alley, with cream cakes and chocolate florentines tumbling along beside me: that's how I saw myself in there, a tiny lost figure rolling away among the pastries, distractedly trying to smooth down its hair, straighten its trousers.

I strolled on past cigar and flower shops, past clothing stores where the mannequins stared out at me with their phony optimism. Then a street branched off to the right; it seemed to consist entirely of wooden shacks. At the corner there was a huge white banner saying: WELCOME DRUGGISTS!

The shacks had been built into the rubble, squatting among burned-out, collapsed façades—but those shacks too were cigar and clothing stores, newsstands, and when I finally came to a snack bar it was closed. I rattled the door handle, turned around, and at last saw a light. I crossed the street toward the light and saw that it came from a church. The high Gothic window had been roughly bricked up, and squeezed into the center of the ugly brickwork was a small, yellow window that had obviously come from a bathroom. The four little panes let through a faint yellow light. I stopped and reflected for a moment: it was unlikely, but just possibly it was warm in there. I walked up some broken steps. The door seemed to be unscathed, it was padded with leather. Inside the church it was not warm. I removed my beret, crept slowly forward between the pews, then saw candles burning in the patched-up transept. I kept on going, although I had discovered that it was even colder in there than outside: it was drafty. There were drafts from all sides. In some places the walls had not even been repaired with bricks, they consisted of sheets of fiberboard simply placed side by side; the adhesive was seeping through, and the fiberboard was beginning to separate into layers and warp. Dirty bulges in the fiberboard were dripping with moisture, and I stood hesitating beside a pillar.

Standing between two windows at a stone altar, between the two candles, was the priest in his white surplice. He was praying with uplifted hands, and although I saw only the priest's back I knew he was feeling cold. For a moment it seemed as if the priest were alone with the open missal, his pale uplifted hands, and shivering back. But in the dimness below the flickering candles I could now make out the fair head of a girl bent intently forward, so far forward that her loose hair had parted on her back into two even strands. Beside her knelt a boy who kept turning from side to side, and in spite of the dim light I could discern in his profile the swollen lids, the gaping mouth, of an imbecile, the inflamed lids, the puffy cheeks, the oddly upthrust mouth; and for the brief moments that his eyes were closed, there was a surprising and challenging expression of contempt on that idiot child's face.

The priest turned, a haggard, pale-faced peasant, his eyes shifted to the column where I stood before he placed his uplifted hands together, spread them again, and murmured some words. Then he turned back, bent over the stone altar, suddenly swung around, and with an almost ridiculous solemnity gave the blessing to the

29

girl and the idiot boy. Strangely enough, although I was in the church I did not feel included. The priest turned back to the altar, put on his biretta, then picked up the chalice and blew out the candle on the right. He walked slowly toward the main altar, genuflected, and disappeared in the deep gloom of the church. I could no longer see him, merely hear the hinges of a door squeaking. Then for a moment I saw the girl in the light: a very gentle profile and a simple devoutness as she stood up, knelt down, then walked up the steps to blow out the other candle. She stood in that soft yellow light, and I could see she was really beautiful; slender and tall with a serene expression, and there was nothing foolish about the way she pursed her lips and blew. Then darkness fell upon her and the boy, and I did not see her again until she emerged into the gray light that fell from the little bricked-in window above. And again I was touched by the way she held her head, moved her neck as she passed me, giving me a calm and searching glance as she left the church. She was beautiful, and I followed her. At the door she genuflected again, pushed open the door, and pulled the idiot after her.

I followed her. She walked in the opposite direction, toward the station, through the desolate street lined only by shacks and rubble, and I noticed her looking back a few times. She was slender, almost thin, seemed scarcely more than eighteen or nineteen, and her patience never wavered as she pulled the boy along.

Now there were more buildings, with only an occasional shack; a number of streetcar tracks converged, and I recognized a part of town I seldom visit. This must be the streetcar depot: I could hear the screeching of wheels behind a clumsily repaired red wall, see in the twilight the blinding flashes from the welding machines, hear the hissing of the oxygen cylinders.

I had been staring so long at the wall that I failed to notice that the girl had stopped. I was now quite close to her and saw that she was standing in front of one of the shacks searching through a bunch of keys. The idiot was looking up into the flat grayness of the sky. Again the girl glanced back at me, and I hesitated for a moment as I passed her until I saw that the shack she had started to open up was a snack bar.

She had already opened the door, and inside in the gray darkness I could see chairs, a counter, the dull gleam of a coffee machine; a stale smell of cold potato pancakes came out through the door, and in the dimness I could see behind smeared glass some meatballs piled up on two platters, some cold chops, and a large green jar of cucumbers floating in vinegar.

The girl looked at me when I stopped. She had removed the steel shutters—and I too looked into her eyes.

"Excuse me," I said, "are you opening up?"

"Yes," she said, and walked past me, carrying the last of the shutters inside, and I could hear her put it down. Although the shutters had been removed, she came back again, looked at me, and I asked:

"Is it all right to come in?"

"Of course," she said, "but it's still cold in there."

"Oh, I don't mind," I said, and went in.

The smell inside was abominable, and I got out my cigarettes and lit one. She had flicked on the switch, and

I was surprised how clean everything looked in the light.

"Funny kind of weather," she said, "for September. By noon it'll be hot again, but now it's really cold."

"Yes," I said, "funny, the mornings are cold."

"I'll light a fire in a second," she said.

Her voice was clear, a bit reedy, and I noticed she was embarrassed.

I merely nodded, crossed over to the wall by the counter, and looked around the room. The walls consisted of bare wooden boards papered with brightly colored cigarette posters: suave men with graying temples holding out their cigarette case to décolleté ladies, smirking invitingly while with the other hand holding a bottle of champagne by the neck—cowboys on horseback with devil-may-care grins on their faces, one hand holding the lasso, the other the cigarette, trailing a cloud of tobacco smoke, as improbably huge as it was blue, that stretched like a silken banner to the horizon of the prairie.

The idiot boy crouched beside the stove, whimpering softly with the cold. He had a sucker in his mouth and was holding the little wooden stick in his hand, maddeningly sucking away at the garish red piece of sugar, while two thin, sticky rivulets, barely visible, ran slowly down the sides of his mouth.

"Bernhard," the girl said gently, bending down to him and carefully wiping the corners of his mouth with her handkerchief. She lifted the lid from the stove, crumpled up some newspaper, threw it in, placed kindling and some broken briquets on top, and held a lighted match to the stove's rusty muzzle.

"Do sit down, won't you?" she said to me.

"Oh thanks," I said, but I didn't sit down.

I felt cold and wanted to stand close to the stove; and in spite of my slight revulsion toward the idiot boy and the stale smells of cheap food, the thought of coffee, of bread and butter, filled me with a pleasant warmth—and I looked down onto the girl's snowy neck, saw the roughly darned stockings on her legs, and watched those gentle movements of her head when she bent down low to see how the fire was coming along.

At first there was only a bit of smoke, until at last I began to hear some crackling; the flames puffed softly, and the smoke subsided. All this time she was kneeling there at my feet, rattling with dirty fingers at the muzzle of the stove and sometimes bending lower to blow, and when she did I could see right down the back of her neck, could see the white, childlike back.

Suddenly she got to her feet, smiled at me, and walked behind the counter. She turned on the tap, washed her hands, and plugged in the coffee machine. I went over to the stove, raised the lid with a hook, and saw that the flames had caught the kindling and were beginning to set the briquets alight. It was really beginning to warm up. The coffee machine was already puffing away, and I could feel my appetite growing. Whenever I have been drinking, I have a big appetite for coffee and breakfast—but I looked with faint disgust at the cold sausages with their wrinkled skin and at the bowls of salad. The girl picked up a metal crate of empty bottles and went out. Being alone with the idiot boy filled me with a strange irritation. The child completely ignored me; it maddened me the way he squatted there so complacently, sucking away at the revolting stick of sugar.

I threw away my cigarette and was startled when the door opened and instead of the girl the priest who had just said Mass appeared. His round, pale peasant face was now topped by a very clean black hat. He said "Good morning," and disappointment fell over his face like a shadow when he saw that the place behind the counter was empty. "Good morning," I said, and thought: Poor bastard. Only now had I recalled that the church where I had been was the Parish Church of the Seven Sorrows, and I was well acquainted with the priest's dossier: his grades had been mediocre, his sermons weren't popular, they lacked drama and his voice was too hoarse. He had not distinguished himself during the war, he had been neither a hero nor a Resistance fighter, no medal had adorned his chest, nor had he been crowned with the invisible crown of martyrdom; there was even a very ordinary disciplinary punishment for breaking curfew to blot his record. But all that wasn't as bad as some strange affair with a woman which, although it turned out to be platonic, had attained a degree of spiritual ardor that gave rise to unease among the hierarchy. The priest of the Seven Sorrows of Mary was one of those whom the Bishop categorized as a typical C-minus priest inclining toward D-plus.

The priest's awkward disappointment was so obvious that I felt embarrassed. I lit another cigarette, said "Good morning" again, and tried to look past that nondescript face. Whenever I see them, priests in their black cassocks, an innocent confidence and at the same time an innocent lack of confidence in their faces, I experience that strange mixture of rage and pity that I also feel toward my children.

The priest was nervously clinking a two-mark piece on the glass counter top. A light flush rose from his neck across his face when the door opened and the girl came in.

"Oh," he said hastily, "I just wanted some cigarettes."

I watched him closely as he reached in carefully with his short white fingers past the chops toward the cigarettes, picked up a red package, tossed the coin onto the counter, and with a barely audible "Good-bye" hastily left the shack.

The girl followed him with her eyes, put down the basket she had been carrying, and I could feel my mouth watering at the sight of those fresh, golden rolls. I gulped down the lukewarm saliva, flicked out my cigarette, and looked for somewhere to sit down. The iron stove was now sending out an intense heat, still somewhat permeated with briquet smoke, and I could taste a faint nausea rising sourly from my stomach.

Outside the streetcars were grinding around the curves as they left the depot, dirty white vehicles linked together in twos and threes, jolting away in fits and starts, their screeching fanning out from a few focal points, like skeins of thread, into yet further channels of white rasping sound.

The water was bubbling softly in the coffee machine, the idiot boy was sucking away at his wooden stick which now held only a thin, transparent layer of pink sugar.

"Coffee?" asked the girl from behind the counter—"would you like some coffee?"

"Yes, please," I said quickly and, as if the tone of my voice had touched her, she turned her calm and lovely face toward me and nodded with a smile while she pushed the cup and saucer under the spout of the machine. She carefully opened the can of coffee, and as she picked up the spoon the marvelous aroma of the ground beans wafted across to me, and she hesitated a moment and asked:

"How much? How much coffee would you like?"

I hurriedly took my money from my pocket, smoothed it out, quickly piled up the coins, went through my pockets again, then counted it all and said:

"Three—I'll need three, three cups."

"Three," she said, and smiled again and added: "Then I'll give you a pot, it's cheaper."

I watched her put four heaped teaspoons of coffee into the little metal drawer, push it in, take away the cup, and replace it with a pot. She calmly adjusted the valves, the machine puffed and bubbled. Steam hissed past her face, and I saw the dark-brown liquid begin to drip into the pot; my heart began to beat a little faster.

Sometimes I think about death and about the moment of transition from this life into that other one, and I try to imagine what will stay with me in that second: the wan face of my wife, the white ear of a priest in the confessional, a few quiet Masses in dim churches, filled with the harmony of the liturgy, and the skin of my children, pink and warm, the schnapps coursing through my veins, and the breakfasts, a few breakfasts—and at this instant, as I was watching the girl adjusting the valves of the coffee machine, I knew that she would be there too. I unbuttoned my coat, threw my beret onto an empty chair.

"Can I also have some rolls?" I asked. "Are they fresh?"

"Of course," she said, "how many would you like? They're really fresh."

"Four," I said, "and some butter too."

"Yes, how much?"

"Oh, an ounce or so."

She took the rolls from the basket, put them on a plate, and began to divide up a half-pound packet of butter with a knife.

"I don't have any scales, may I make it a bit more? Two ounces? Then I could do it with the knife."

"Yes," I said, "sure," and it was quite clear that what she put beside the rolls was more than two ounces; it was the biggest of the four quarters which she had divided the package into.

She carefully removed the paper from the butter and came over to me carrying the tray.

She held the tray up close to my face because she was trying to spread a napkin with her free hand, and I helped her by unfolding the napkin, and for a moment I could smell her hands: her hands smelled good.

"There you are," she said.

"Thank you," I said.

I poured myself a cup, added some sugar, stirred the coffee, and drank. The coffee was hot and very good. Only my wife can make coffee like that, but I so rarely have coffee at home, and I wondered how long it had been since I had had such good coffee. I took several gulps and immediately felt my spirits revive. "Marvelous," I called out to the girl, "your coffee's marvelous!" She smiled, nodded, and I suddenly realized how much I liked looking at her. Her presence filled me with a sense of relaxation and well-being.

"First time anybody's told me my coffee's that good."

"Well, it is," I said.

Later I heard the clink of empty bottles in the metal crate outside, the milkman came in carrying full bottles, and she calmly checked them off with her white fingers: milk, chocolate, yogurt, and cream. It was getting hot in the shack, and the idiot boy was still sitting there holding the bare sucker stick in his mouth, uttering occasional sounds, shreds of words all starting with z and seeming to contain a tune—*zu zu-za za-zozu*, a wild secret rhythm filled this sibilant babble, and a grin spread over the idiot's face whenever the girl turned toward him.

Some streetcar repairmen came in, removed the protective goggles from their eyes, sat down, drank milk through straws out of bottles; I noticed the city crest embroidered on their coveralls. Outside things were livening up, the long rows of streetcars had disappeared, and now grimy white vehicles were screeching past spaced at regular intervals.

I thought about Käte, my wife, and that I would be with her that evening. But first I had to raise some money, find a room. It's not easy to raise money, and I wished there were someone who would give it to me right away. But in a city like ours, a city of three hundred thousand inhabitants, it's not easy to find someone who will give you money just for the asking. I did know a few people I found it easier to ask, and I intended to go and see them; maybe at the same time I could look in at the hotels and try and find a room.

I had finished my coffee, it must have been close to seven. Tobacco smoke filled the shack, and a disabled veteran, tired and unshaven, who had come hobbling in with a smile, sat up front by the stove, drinking coffee and feeding the idiot with cheese sandwiches that he unwrapped from some newspaper.

Calmly, a dishcloth in her hand, taking money, giving change, smiling and nodding, the girl stood near the front, pressing the lever of the coffee machine, drying the bottles with a cloth as she took them out of the hot water. Everything she did seemed so easy, so effortless, although often for minutes at a time impatient customers would press around the counter. She poured hot milk, cold chocolate, hot chocolate, let the steam from the coffee machine hiss past her face, fished pickles out of the cloudy jar with wooden tongs—and suddenly the shack was empty. Only a fat, pasty-faced young fellow remained in front of the counter, holding a pickle in one hand and a cold chop in the other. He rapidly polished off both, lit a cigarette, and slowly picked out some money from the loose change he seemed to be carrying in his pocket; and his brand-new suit, only slightly wrinkled, and his tie, suddenly made me aware that outside it was a day of rest, that in the city Sunday was just beginning, and I remembered how hard it is to raise money on a Sunday.

Then the young fellow went out too, leaving only the unshaven veteran who with unwavering patience continued to feed bits of cheese sandwich into the idiot's mouth while softly imitating the child's sounds, *zu zu-za za-zozo*, although his own babbling was not filled with the same wild, fascinating rhythm. My eyes rested on the idiot as he munched the bits of bread. The girl leaned against the wall of the shack, watching them. She was drinking hot milk from a mug and slowly biting off mouthfuls of dry roll. All was quiet and peaceful now, and I sensed an acute irritation mounting in me.

"The bill, please," I called abruptly, and got up.

I felt something like embarrassment when the disabled man gave me a cool, scrutinizing glance. The idiot also turned toward me, but his unfocused blue gaze strayed past me, and into the silence the girl said softly:

"That'll do, Father, I think Bernhard's had enough."

She took the note from my hand, dropped it into a cigar box under the counter, and slowly counted out my change onto the glass top, and when I pushed a tip across the glass to her she took it with a murmured "Thank you" and raised the mug to her lips to drink some milk. Even in broad daylight she was beautiful, and I hesitated a moment before leaving. I could have stayed there for hours, just sitting and waiting: I turned my back on the three of them and paused, then pulled myself together, muttered "Good-bye," and hurried out.

Outside the door, two young fellows in white shirts were busy unrolling a banner and fastening it to two wooden poles. Flowers had been scattered on the street, and I waited for a moment until the banner was completely unrolled, and I could read the inscription, red letters on a white ground: HAIL OUR PASTORAL LEADER!

I lit a cigarette and turned slowly in the direction of the city to raise some money and find a room for the night.

4

When I go to the tap to fill my pail, I can't help seeing my face in the mirror: a skinny woman who has come to know the bitterness of life. My hair is still thick, and the traces of gray at my temples that give my fair hair a silvery sheen are merely a token of my grief over the two babies who, my father confessor tells me, I should pray to. They were the same age as Franz is now, were just beginning to sit up in bed, to try to talk to me. They never played in flowery meadows, but sometimes I see them in a flowery meadow, and my grief is mingled with certain satisfaction—satisfaction that these two children have been spared from life. And yet I see two other, imaginary, beings growing up, changing year by year, almost month by month. They resemble what the babies might have become. In the eyes of these two other children, standing in the mirror behind my face and waving to me, is a wisdom that I recognize without applying it. For in the wistful smiling eyes of these two children appearing in the depths of the mirror, in a silvery twilight—in their eyes I see patience, infinite patience, and I—I am not patient, I refuse to give up the battle they are counseling me not to begin.

My pail takes a long time to fill, and as soon as the gurgling sounds higher, higher and higher, alarmingly thin, as soon as I hear the tinny implement of my daily battle filling up, my eyes return from the background of the mirror and rest for another second on my face: the cheekbones are a bit prominent because I am getting too thin, the pallor of my face is turning sallow, and I wonder whether I shouldn't change the color of my lipstick for this evening, maybe use a brighter red.

How many thousand times must my hands have gone through these motions! Without looking I can hear that the pail is full, I turn off the water, my hands quickly grasp the handle, and I can feel my arm muscles tightening as I swing the heavy pail down onto the floor.

I put my ear to the door of the cubicle we have partitioned off with plywood, to make sure Franz is still asleep.

Then I start my battle, my battle against dirt. Where I derive the hope of ever subduing it, I don't know. I put off the assault a bit, comb my hair without looking in the mirror, clear away the breakfast dishes, and light the half-cigarette that was lying in the cupboard between my prayer book and the coffee jar.

Next door they have woken up. Through the thin wall I can distinctly hear the hissing of the gas flame, the early-morning giggling, and those detested voices embark on their conversation. He must still be in bed, his muttering is unintelligible, and I can make out her words only when she is not facing away.

"... last Sunday eight real ... buy some new rubbers ... when do we get paid? ..."

He seems to be reading the movie ads to her, for suddenly I hear her say: "Let's go there."

So they'll be going out, to a movie, they'll be going to a bar, and I am beginning to regret a little that I have a date with Fred, for this evening it will be quiet, at least next door. But Fred is already on his way, probably trying to get a room and some money, and it's too late now to cancel our date. And I've finished my cigarette.

The moment I move the cupboard, bits of loose plaster crumble from the wall toward me—fragments come pattering down between the cupboard legs, spreading out quickly over the floor, a chalky avalanche, powdery and dry, already starting to disintegrate. Sometimes a whole slab will slide down, its cracks rapidly widening, and when I move the cupboard the obstruction behind it breaks up and descends with muffled thunder, while a chalky cloud tells me that a day of exceptional battle has dawned. Dust settles on every object in the room, a fine, chalky powder that obliges me to go over everything a second time with my duster. It crunches under my feet, and through the thin wall of the cubicle I can hear the baby coughing, trying to get rid of that horrible dust in his throat. Despair rises in me like a physical pain, my throat closes on a knot of anger that I try to swallow. I choke it down, and a mixture of dust, tears, and despair slides into my stomach, and now I really take up the battle. My face twitching, I sweep up the pieces after opening the window, then with my duster I carefully wipe every surface. Finally I dip the floor cloth in the water. As soon as I have tried to clean one square yard I have to rinse out the floor cloth, a milky cloud immediately begins to spread through the clear water. After the third square yard the water has thickened, and when I empty the pail a disgusting chalky sediment stays behind that I scrape out with my hands and rinse away. And again have to fill the pail.

Gazing past my face, my eyes look into the mirror, and I can see them, my two babies, Regina and Robert, twins I bore only to see them die. It was Fred's hands that cut the umbilical cords, that boiled the instruments, rested on my forehead, while I screamed in labor. He kept the stove going, rolled cigarettes for us both, and was a deserter, and sometimes I think I have loved him only since I realized how much he despises the law. He lifted me in his arms, carried me down into the cellar, and was beside me when I first put them to my breast, down in the airless chill of the cellar, by the soft light of a candle, with Clemens sitting on his little chair looking at a picture book and the shells hurtling over our building.

But the ominous gurgling recalls me to my battle against the dirt, and as once again I swing the pail down onto the floor I see that the places I had just washed have dried and reveal that loathsome film of white chalk, hideous patches which I know can never be eradicated. This pallid nothingness kills my good intentions, wears down my strength, and the encouragement provided by the sight of the clean water in my pail is minimal.

Again and again I lift the empty container under the slowly running tap, my eyes seize upon the unfocused, milky distance in the back of the mirror—and I see the bodies of my two children, covered with swollen bedbug bites, bitten all over by lice, and I feel sick to my stomach at the thought of that vast army of vermin mobilized by war. Billions of lice and bedbugs, of mosquitoes and fleas, are on the march as soon as war breaks out, following the silent command that tells them there's a feast to be had.

Oh I know, and I'm not likely to forget! I know that death came to my children from the lice, that we were sold a totally useless remedy from a factory run by the cousin of the Minister of Health, while the good, the effective, remedy was withheld. Oh I know, and I'm not likely to forget, for I see them, back there in the mirror, my two babies, vermin-ridden and ugly, feverish and crying, their little bodies swollen from useless injections. And I turn off the tap without lifting the pail, for today is Sunday, and I am going to treat myself to a rest in the battle against the dirt that the war has set in motion.

And I see Fred's face, inexorably aging, eroded by a life that would be useless, and always would have been useless, without the love it inspires in me. The face of a man seized at an early age by indifference toward everything that other men are determined to take seriously. I see him often, very often, more often than ever now that he no longer lives with us.

In the mirror I am smiling, I am amazed to see my own smile, of which I know nothing, I listen to the gurgling in the tap getting higher and higher. I fail to bring back my gaze from the mirror, to direct it to my face, my real face, which I know is not smiling.

Beyond my face I see women—yellow women doing their laundry beside sluggish rivers, hear their singing— I see black women digging in sunbaked earth, hear the drumming, meaningless yet fascinating, of idle men in the background; I see brown women grinding grain in stone troughs, carrying infants on their backs, while the men squat stupidly around a fire smoking their pipes —and my white sisters in the tenements of London, New York, and Berlin, in the dark canyons of Paris back streets—bitter faces, listening in terror for a drunkard's shouts. And looking past the mirror I see the hideous army advance, the unknown, unsung mobilization of vermin bringing death to my children.

But the pail is long since full, and although it is Sunday I must clean, I must battle the dirt.

For years I have been battling the dirt of this single room; I fill the pails, wring out the cloths, pour the dirty water down the drain, and I suppose my battle will be won when I have scraped out, rinsed out, as much chalky sediment as the masons blithely plastered into the walls of this room sixty years ago.

My eyes often look into the mirror, as often as I have to fill the pail, and when my eyes return from back there they settle in front on my own face that, lifeless and detached, has been watching the invisible game, and then I sometimes see a smile on it, a smile that must have fallen onto it from the faces of the babies, and remained there. Or I see an expression of fierce determination, of hatred and a ruthlessness that fills me with pride rather than alarm, the ruthlessness of a face that will never forget.

But today is Sunday, and I'm going to be with Fred. The baby is asleep, Clemens has gone off to the procession with Carla, and from the courtyard I can hear the echoes of three church services, two concerts, one lecture, and the husky singing of a Negro that cuts through it all and is the only thing that touches my heart.

... and he never said a mumbling word ...

Maybe Fred will raise some money and we'll go dancing. I'll buy a new lipstick, buy it on credit from the landlady downstairs. And it would be nice if Fred would take me dancing. I can still hear the gentle, husky cry of the Negro, hear it through two watery sermons, and I can feel my hatred mounting, hatred for those voices whose prattle seeps into me like slow decay.

... they nailed him to the cross, nailed him to the cross.

Yes, today is Sunday, and our room is filled with the smell of the roast, and this smell could make me weep,

weep at the delight of the children, who so seldom get any meat.

> ... *and he never said a mumbling word*, sings the Negro,
> ... *and never said a word.*

5

I went back to the railway station, got some change at a snack counter, and decided to take the easy way out because it was Sunday. I was too tired and too desperate to go and see all those people I could ask for money, so I thought I would phone them, those that had a phone. Sometimes on the phone I manage to imbue my voice with that casual note that enhances one's credit, the secret being that when genuine need is audible in a voice, visible in a face, it tightens the purse strings.

A phone booth at the station was free, and I went in, jotted down the numbers of a few hotels, and pulled out my notebook to look up the numbers of the people I could ask for money. I had plenty of change in my pocket, and I hesitated a bit longer, looked at the ancient, soiled rate schedule on the walls of the booth, the defaced "Instructions for Use," and reluctantly dropped the first two coins in the slot. Much as I try, much as this constant attempt to borrow money depresses me and is gradually turning into a nightmare,

I never regret having been drunk. I dialed the number of the man most likely to give me something, yet his refusal would also make everything much worse because of my greater reluctance to ask all the others. So I let the two coins sit there in the bowels of the instrument, pressed down the cradle once more, and waited a bit. Sweat was gathering on my forehead, it made my shirt stick to the back of my neck, and I realized how much I depended on getting some money.

Outside the booth I saw the shadow of a man who seemed to be waiting, and I was about to press the other button to let my money roll out again when the next booth became free and the shadow outside my door disappeared. I still hesitated. Above my head the trains rumbled in and out, and way off I could hear the voice of the announcer. I wiped away the sweat and told myself that never in so short a time would I be able to scrape up the money I needed to be with Käte.

I was too ashamed to pray that the man I was calling would give me money right away, so I pulled myself together, dialed the number once more, and took my left hand off the cradle so I wouldn't be able to press it down again; when I had dialed the last digit there was a moment's silence followed by the buzzing tone, and I could visualize Serge's library where the phone was now ringing. I could see all those books of his, the tasteful etchings on the walls, and the stained-glass window depicting Saint Cassius. I remembered the banner I had just seen: HAIL OUR PASTORAL LEADER! and I realized it was Procession Day, of course, and that Serge was probably not home. I was sweating more heavily than ever, had probably failed to hear Serge's voice the first time, for he said very impatiently: "Hello, who is it?"

At the tone of his voice all my courage melted away, and a great deal went through my head in a single second: whether, when I asked him for money, he would be able to differentiate between me his employee and me the borrower, and I said as loud as I could: "It's Bogner," wiped the cold sweat away with my left hand but listened very carefully for Serge's voice, and I shall never forget my relief when I heard his voice take on a friendlier tone.

"Oh, it's you," he said. "Why didn't you speak up?"

"I was scared," I said.

He was silent, and I could hear the trains rumbling, the voice of the announcer above my head, and could see a woman's shadow outside my door. I examined my handkerchief. It was soiled and damp. Serge's voice hit me between the eyes when he said:

"Well, how much do you need?"

Through the phone I could now hear the beautiful, somber bells from the Church of the Epiphany as they set up a booming resonance in the receiver, and I said in a low voice: "Fifty."

"How much?"

"Fifty," I said, still trembling from the blow he had not intended to inflict. But that's the way it is: when a person hears me, sees me, he knows at once that I'm going to ask him for money.

"What time is it?" he asked.

I opened the door of my booth, first looked into the grumpy face of an elderly woman who was standing there shaking her head, then above the banner of the Druggists' Federation I saw the station clock and said into the receiver:

"Seven-thirty."

Serge was silent again, I could hear the somber, enticing resonance of the church bells in the receiver, and from outside, above the noises of the station, the bells of the cathedral, and Serge said:

"Come around at ten."

I was afraid he would hang up right away, and said hurriedly:

"Hello, sir, hello . . ."

"Yes, what is it?"

"Can I count on it?"

"You can," he said. "Good-bye."

And I heard him put back his receiver, replaced mine, and opened the door of the booth.

I decided to save the cost of phone calls and walked slowly into the city to look for a room. But it was very hard to get a room. Because of the big procession there were a lot of visitors in town, and the stream of foreign tourists had not let up either, and conventions had recently brought intellectuals from all over the country into the city. It had become popular for surgeons, philatelists, and charity organizations to gather every year in the shadow of the cathedral. They filled the hotels, drove up the prices, used up their expense accounts.

Now the druggists were here, and there seemed to be a great number of druggists around.

They showed up everywhere, wearing little red flags on their lapels, the badge of their association. The early-morning chill did not seem to affect their good spirits, they exchanged happy shoptalk on buses and streetcars, dashed off to committee meetings and board elections, and seemed determined to occupy every hotel in the medium-price range for at least a week. There really were a great many druggists around, and many of them had been joined by their wives for the weekend, making it especially hard to find double rooms. The association had also mounted an exhibition, and there were banners inviting one to visit this magnificent display of hygiene products. Every now and then groups of the faithful would appear in the center of the city en route to the assembly point of the procession: a priest surrounded by large gilded baroque lanterns and red-robed choir-boys, men and women in their Sunday best.

A toothpaste manufacturer had rented a dirigible that was releasing tiny white parachutes. The parachutes floated slowly earthward carrying packages of tooth-paste onto the city, and on the embankment a huge cannon was firing off balloons which bore the name of the competition. Further surprises had been announced, and there were rumors that the advertising gag on the part of a large rubber-goods manufacturer had been sabotaged by the Church.

When I started for Serge's at ten o'clock I still hadn't found a room, and my head was buzzing with the replies of pale landladies and the surly growls of bleary-eyed night porters. The dirigible had suddenly vanished, and the cannon banging away on the embankment could no longer be heard, and when I recognized the hymn tunes coming from the southern part of the city I knew the procession was now under way.

Serge's housekeeper showed me into the library. Before I could sit down he came in through the bedroom door, and I saw at once that he had money in his hand. I saw one green bank note, one blue one, and in the other, slightly cupped palm, were some coins. I stared at the floor, waiting for his shadow to fall over me, then looked up, and the expression on my face made him say:

"Come on, it can't be that bad."

I didn't contradict him.

"Here you are," he said. I held out my upturned palms, he placed the two bank notes in my right hand, piled some coins on top, and said:

"Thirty-five, that's the best I can do!"

"Oh, thanks," I said.

I looked at him and tried to smile, but an uncontrollable sob came up like a belch. No doubt the whole thing embarrassed him. His neatly brushed cassock, his well-manicured hands, his closely shaven cheeks, all this made me conscious of the shabbiness of our apartment, the poverty which we have been breathing in for the last ten years like white dust that can be neither tasted nor felt—that invisible, indefinable, but genuine dust of poverty that has settled in my lungs, my heart, my brain, that dominates the blood as it circulates in my body and that now made me short of breath: I had to cough and gasp for air.

"Well, then," I said with an effort, "good-bye and thanks a lot."

"My regards to your wife."

"Thank you," I said.

We shook hands, and I walked to the door. When I turned around I saw that behind my back he had raised his hand in a blessing, and that's how I saw him standing there before I closed the door: his arms hanging helplessly at his sides, his face beet-red. Outside it was chilly, and I turned up my coat collar. I walked slowly toward the center of town in the distance and could already hear the sound of hymns, the drawn-out notes of the trombones, the voices of women singing that were suddenly drowned out by the vigorous voices of a male choir. Gusts of wind brought the singing closer, scrambled harmonies mixed with the dust whirled up by the wind in the ruins. Each time the dust blew into my face I was struck by the emotionalism of the singing. But this singing suddenly broke off, and a few yards farther on I found myself on the street along which the procession happened to be passing. There weren't too many people on the sidewalks, and I stood there and waited.

Robed in the red of the martyrs, the Bishop walked all alone between the bearers of the Sacrament and the male choral society. The flushed faces of the singers looked baffled, almost stupid, as if they were still listening to the subdued bellowing they had just broken off.

The Bishop was very tall and slim, and his thick white hair puffed out from under his close-fitting red skullcap. He held himself very erect, his hands were folded, and I could see he was not praying although his hands were folded and his eyes were gazing straight ahead. The gold cross on his breast swung gently back and forth to the rhythm of his stride. The Bishop had a lordly, swinging stride, and at every step he extended his foot in its red morocco slipper as if in a mild varia-tion of the goose step. The Bishop had been an army officer. His ascetic face was photogenic. It served very nicely as a cover photo for religious magazines.

The members of the cathedral chapter followed at a short distance. Of these only two had the good fortune to possess ascetic faces; all the others were stout, either very pale or very red in the face, and their faces bore an expression of indignation of undeterminable origin.

The richly embroidered baroque canopy was carried by four men in tuxedos, and under the canopy walked the diocesan bishop with the monstrance. Although the Host was very large I could hardly see it, but I knelt down, crossed myself, and had the fleeting sensation of being a hypocrite until I remembered that God was innocent and that it was not hypocrisy to kneel before Him. Almost everyone along the sidewalks knelt down, only one very young man wearing a green corduroy jacket and a beret remained standing without removing his beret or his hands from his pockets. I was glad that at least he wasn't smoking. A white-haired man ap-proached him from behind, whispered something, and the young man, with a shrug of the shoulders, removed his beret and held it in front of him, but he didn't kneel down.

I suddenly felt very sad again, and my eyes followed the Sacrament-bearers as they proceeded down the wide street, where the kneeling, rising, and dusting off of trouser legs was now traveling like a wave. After the Sacrament-bearers came a group of some twenty men in tuxedos. The suits were all clean, well tailored, except for two of the men whose suits did not fit, and I saw at once that they were workingmen. It must be terrible for them to walk among the others whose suits fitted well because they were their own. Obviously the workingmen had borrowed their black suits. It is well known that the Bishop has a highly developed social consciousness, and no doubt he had insisted that there should also be some workingmen among the canopy-bearers.

A group of monks passed by. They were very impressive. Their black vestments over their cream-colored habits, the neatly shaved tonsures on the bowed heads: it was all very impressive. And the monks didn't have to fold their hands, they could hide them in their wide sleeves. The group moved along, heads bowed in pensive mood, quite silent, not too fast, not too slow, in the measured tread of spirituality. The wide collars, the long robes, and the beautiful harmony of black and white, all that endowed them with something that was both youthful and intelligent, and the sight might have made me wish to be one of their order. But I know some of them and am aware that in the uniform of secular priests they look no better than these others.

The academics, numbering almost a hundred, looked very intelligent, at least some of them did. A few of the faces bore a look of somewhat pained intelligence. Most of them were in tuxedos, but some were wearing ordinary dark-gray suits.

Then came the various parish priests of the city, flanked by great baroque lanterns, and I could see how difficult it is to cut a good figure in the baroque vestments of a secular priest. Most of the priests were not lucky enough to look like ascetics, some were very stout and looked quite robust. And most of the people lining the street looked in poor health, harassed, and a bit critical.

The members of student corps all wore gaily colored caps, gaily colored sashes, and those walking in the middle each carried a gaily colored flag that hung down heavy and silken. There were seven or eight ranks of three students in succession, and the group as a whole was the most gaily colored I had ever seen. The faces of the students were very solemn, and they all stared straight ahead without blinking, apparently at some very remote and very fascinating goal, and not one of them seemed aware that they looked ridiculous. One of them—wearing a blue, red, and green cap— had sweat pouring down his face although it was not very warm. But he made no move to wipe off the sweat, and he looked not so much ridiculous as thoroughly unhappy. I imagined that there would probably be something like a court of honor, and that he would be expelled for insubordinate sweating during the procession, and that this might mean the end of his career.

And in fact he did give the impression of someone who had lost his chance in life, and all the others, who were not sweating, looked as though they really never would give him another chance.

A large group of schoolchildren came by, singing much too fast, a little disjointedly, and it sounded almost like canon-singing, for from the rear the words sung by those at the head of the group always resounded loud and clear exactly three seconds later. A few young teachers in brand-new tuxedos, and two young clerics in lace surplices, ran back and forth attempting to restore synchronization in the singing as they waved their arms about, trying to regulate the tempo and signal the laws of harmony to those at the rear. But it was all quite useless.

Suddenly my head swam, and I no longer saw either the people in the procession or the spectators. The sector I had in view had shrunk, as if compressed, and through a haze of flickering gray I saw only them, my two children, Clemens and Carla, the boy very pale, looking tall in his blue suit, wearing the green sprig of a First Communicant in his buttonhole and carrying a candle; his dear, solemn child's face was pale and composed, and my daughter, who has my dark hair, my round face and slight build, was smiling a little. Although I seemed far away from them, I saw them quite clearly, saw into that part of my life as into the life of a stranger that I had been burdened with. And in these children of mine, slowly marching along and solemnly carrying their candles across my minute field of vision

—in them I saw what I always thought I knew but only knew now: that we are poor.

I was caught up in the eddying crowds that followed on the heels of the procession and were determined to attend the concluding service in the cathedral. For a while I made futile efforts to break out to either side. I was too tired to clear my way. I let myself drift, slowly edging toward the outside. The people were disgusting, and I began to hate them. As long as I can remember I have always had an aversion toward corporal punishment. It always caused me pain when someone was beaten in my presence, and whenever I was a witness I tried to prevent it. Even among prisoners of war. It landed me in a lot of trouble and danger, the fact that I couldn't bear to see prisoners being flogged, but there was nothing I could do about my revulsion, even if I had wanted to. I couldn't bear to watch someone being beaten or maltreated, and I intervened not because I felt pity, much less love, but simply because I found it unbearable.

During the last few months, though, I have often had the urge to strike someone in the face, and sometimes I even strike my children because I was irritated by their noise when I came home tired from work. I would hit them hard, very hard, knowing that what they were suffering through me was unjust, and it scared me to find I was losing my self-control.

I am often overcome, very suddenly, by the wild desire to hit someone in the face: the thin woman now walking beside me in the crowd, so close that I could smell her sour, stale odor. Her face was a grimace of hatred, and she screamed at her husband who was walking ahead of us, a quiet-seeming, narrow-shouldered figure wearing a green felt hat: "Go on, hurry up, get going, we'll be late for Mass!"

I managed to push my way over to the far right and was able to extricate myself from the current. I stopped in front of the window of a shoe store and let the crowd stream past. I felt for the money in my pocket, counted the bank notes and coins without taking them out, and made sure that nothing was missing.

I would have liked a cup of coffee, but I had to be careful with the money.

Suddenly the street was empty, and now I could see only the dirt, the trampled flowers, the finely ground plaster dust, and the banners hanging askew between old streetcar poles. In black and white they displayed the first lines of hymns:

Praise ye the Lord.
Holy Mother, bless our vows.

And some of the banners bore symbols: lambs and chalices, palm branches, hearts and anchors.

I lit a cigarette and strolled toward the northern end of the city. From a distance the songs of the procession could still be heard, but a few minutes later all was quiet, and I knew the procession had reached the cathedral. A Sunday-morning movie was just emptying, and I found myself among a group of young intellectuals who had already begun to discuss the film. They

were wearing trench coats and berets and had formed
a group around a very pretty girl in a bright-green
sweater and cutoff American army khakis:

". . . impressive banality. . . ."

". . . but the means. . . ."

". . . Kafka. . . ."

I couldn't get my kids out of my mind. It was as if
I could see them with closed eyes: my children, the boy
all of thirteen, the girl eleven; pale creatures both of
them, destined for the treadmill. The two older ones
loved to sing, but I had forbidden them to do so when
I was at home. Their high spirits got on my nerves, their
noise, and I had beaten them, I, the very person who
had never been able to stand the sight of corporal punishment. I had struck them in the face, on their behinds,
because I wanted quiet, peace and quiet in the evenings
when I came home from work.

From the cathedral came the sound of singing, the
wind was wafting waves of musical religiosity over
me, and I walked past the railway station. I saw a group
of men in white overalls removing the banners with the
religious symbols from the flagpoles and hanging up
new ones that said: GERMAN DRUGGISTS' FEDERATION.
VISIT THE EXHIBITION! MANY FREE SAMPLES!

Where would I be without my druggist?

Slowly, unwittingly, I strolled toward the Church
of the Seven Sorrows of Mary, walked past the main
door and, without looking up, to the snack booth where
I had had my breakfast that morning. It was almost as
if I had counted my steps that morning, as if some
mysterious rhythm controlling my leg muscles were

forcing me to stop and look up—and I looked to the right, through a gap in the curtain saw the platter with the chops, the large colored cigarette posters, and I approached the door, opened it, and went in. It was quiet inside, and I immediately sensed that she wasn't there. The idiot wasn't there either. In the corner sat a streetcar repairman spooning up his soup, at the next table a couple with packets of sandwiches and cups of coffee, and behind the counter the disabled veteran got up, looked at me, and seemed to recognize me: the corners of his mouth twitched slightly. The streetcar repairman and the couple also looked at me.

"What can I do for you?" said the veteran.

"Cigarettes, five," I muttered, "the red pack."

Wearily I fished for a coin in my pocket, placed it carefully on the glass counter, pocketed the cigarettes the veteran had handed me, said "Thank you," and waited.

I looked slowly around. They were still staring at me: the streetcar repairman, holding his spoon halfway between mouth and plate—I could see the yellow soup dripping down—and the couple paused in their chewing, the husband with his mouth open, the wife with hers closed. Then I looked at the veteran: he was smiling; under his swarthy, unshaven skin I recognized her face.

The room was very quiet, and into the silence he asked: "Are you looking for someone?"

I shook my head, turned toward the door, paused for a moment, and could feel the eyes of the others on my back before I left. The street was still empty when I stepped out.

A drunk came staggering out of the dark underpass leading beyond the railway station. His clumsy, weaving gait was aimed straight at me, and when he was close I recognized the little flag of the druggists on his lapel. He halted in front of me, grabbed my coat button, and belched the sour smell of beer into my face:

"Where would you be without your druggist?" he mumbled.

"Nowhere," I said softly, "without my druggist I am nowhere."

"There you are!" he said contemptuously, let go of me, and staggered on.

I walked slowly into the dark underpass.

Behind the station, all was quiet. The bittersweet odor of ground cocoa beans and the smell of caramel hung over the entire area. A large chocolate factory covers three city blocks with its buildings and walkways, lending this part of town a veneer of gloom not in keeping with its appetizing products. This is where the poor live, the few hotels in this area are cheap, and the tourist bureau avoids sending visitors here for fear of their being repelled by so much poverty. The narrow streets were filled with cooking smells: the odor of steamed cabbage, and the intoxicating smells of large roasts. Children stood around with suckers in their mouths, through open windows I glimpsed shirt-sleeved men playing cards, and on the fire-blackened wall of a ruined building I saw a large, grimy sign displaying a pointing black hand, and beneath the black hand were the words: HOLLAND HOUSE: ROOMS, HOME COOKING, DANCING SUNDAYS.

I followed the direction of the black hand, found another black hand at the corner with the inscription: HOLL. HOUSE, ACROSS THE STREET; and when I raised my eyes and looked at the building opposite, red brick encrusted with the black smoke from the chocolate factory, I knew that the druggists had not penetrated this far.

6

I am invariably surprised at the agitation that seizes me whenever I hear Fred's voice on the phone: his voice is husky, rather tired, and has a nuance of authority that makes him sound like a stranger and adds to my agitation. That's how I heard him speak during the war from Odessa, from Sebastopol, from countless taverns when he was beginning to get drunk, and how often my heart trembled as I lifted the receiver and over the line heard him pressing the pay button and the coins falling to complete the connection. The hum of the silent exchange before he spoke, his cough, the tenderness his voice can express over the phone.

When I came downstairs the landlady was sitting in her usual corner on the sofa, surrounded by shabby furniture, the desk covered with cartons of soap, boxes of contraceptives, and little wooden cases where she kept her most expensive cosmetics. The room was filled with the odor of women's overheated hair coming from the cubicles up front, that acrid, horrible odor of an entire Saturday's overheated hair. Mrs. Röder, however, was frowzy, her hair unkempt, she held the library novel open without reading it because she was watching me as I held the receiver to my ear. Then without looking she reached into the corner behind the sofa, fished out the schnapps bottle, and filled her glass without taking her tired eyes off me.

"Hello, Fred," I said.

"Käte," he said, "I've got a room and some money."

"Oh, good."

"When are you coming?"

"At five. I want to bake a cake for the children. Are we going dancing?"

"Sure, if you like. There's dancing right here in the hotel."

"Where are you?"

"At the Holland House."

"Where's that?"

"It's north of the station—walk along Station Street, then at the corner you'll see a sign with a black hand. Just follow the pointing finger. How are the kids?"

"Fine."

"I've got some chocolate for them, and we'll buy them some balloons, and I'd like to pay for some ice cream for them too. I'll give you some money for them, and tell them I'm sorry I—I smacked them. I was wrong."

"I can't tell them that, Fred," I said.

"Why not?"

"Because they'll cry."

"Let them cry, but they have to know I'm sorry. It's very important to me. Please don't forget."

I didn't know what to tell him. I watched the landlady fill her second glass with an experienced gesture,
raise the glass to her lips, let the schnapps roll slowly
around her tongue, and I saw the expression of mild
disgust in her face as the schnapps went down her
throat.

"Käte," said Fred.

"Yes?"

"Tell the kids everything, please don't forget, and
tell them about the chocolate, the balloons, and the ice
cream. Promise me."

"I can't," I said, "they're so happy today because
they were allowed to march in the procession. I don't
want to remind them of the beatings. I'll tell them
later, sometime when we're talking about you."

"Do you talk about me?"

"Yes, they ask me where you are, and I say you're
sick."

"Am I sick?"

"Yes, you're sick."

He was silent, and I could hear his breathing in the
receiver. The landlady winked at me and nodded her
head vigorously.

"Maybe you're right, maybe I really am sick. See
you at five, then. The sign with the black hand at
the corner of Station Street. I have enough money,
and we'll go dancing. Good-bye, my love."

"Good-bye." I slowly replaced the receiver and
saw the landlady putting another glass on the table.

"Come along, girl," she said quietly. "Have a drink."

There had been a time when I would feel defiant,

and I would go down to complain to her about the conditions of our room. But she defeated me every time with her overwhelming lethargy; she would pour me a drink and let the wisdom of her tired eyes have its effect on me. Moreover, she knew how to persuade me that to renovate the room would cost more than three years' rent. It is from her that I learned to drink schnapps. At first I found the brandy painful, and I asked for a liqueur. "A liqueur!" she said. "Who on earth wants to drink liqueur?" Meanwhile I have long been convinced she is right: this brandy is good.

"Come along now, girl. Have a drink."

I sat down opposite her, she looked at me with the fixed stare of a drunk, and my gaze traveled past her face and fell on a stack of striped cartons with the words: GRISS RUBBER. QUALITY GOODS. LOOK FOR THE STORK TRADEMARK.

"Here's to you," she said, and I raised my glass and said "You too," let the pleasantly stinging brandy flow into me, and at that moment I understood, understood the men who are drunkards, understood Fred, and all those others who have ever been drinkers.

"Poor child," she said, as she poured me another glass with a speed that surprised me. "Don't ever come here again and complain. There's no cure for poverty. Send the kids down to me this afternoon, they can play here. Are you going out?"

"Yes," I said, "I am, but I've asked a young man to stay with the children."

"Overnight?"

"Yes, overnight."

A wan grin puffed up her face for a second like a
yellow sponge, then it collapsed again.

"Oh I see, then take up some empty boxes for them."

"Oh thanks," I said.

Her husband had been a broker and had left her
three buildings, the hairdressing business, and a col-
lection of boxes.

"Shall we have another?"

"Oh no thanks," I said.

Her trembling hands become steady as soon as they
touch the bottle, and those movements are filled with a
tenderness that frightens me. She refilled my glass too.

"Please," I said, "no more for me."

"Then I'll drink it," she said, and suddenly she looked
at me sharply, narrowing her eyes, and asked:

"Are you pregnant, my child?"

I was startled. Sometimes I think I actually am, but
I don't know yet for sure. I shook my head.

"Poor child," she said, "that's going to be tough for
you. Another baby."

"I don't know," I said uncertainly.

"You must change the color of your lipstick, child."
She gave me another sharp look, got up and, maneuver-
ing her heavy body in the colorful robe, worked her
way out from among chair, sofa, and desk. "Come with
me."

I followed her into the shop: the smell of overheated
hair, of perfumed spray, hung thickly like a cloud, and
in the half-light of the curtained room I could see the
permanent-wave machines, the driers, a pale glimmer
of nickel in the leaden light of Sunday afternoon.

71

"Come on in!"

She rummaged in a drawer in which hair curlers, loose lipsticks, and colored compacts were lying around. She picked up a lipstick, held it out to me, and said: "Try this one." I unscrewed the metal top, saw the dark-red stick wind itself out like a rigid worm.

"That dark?" I asked.

"Yes, that dark. Go ahead, put some on."

These mirrors down here are quite different. They prevent you from looking into the background, hold your face up front, very close to the surface, more beautiful than it is—and I parted my lips, leaned forward, and carefully applied the dark red. But my eyes are not used to these mirrors, my eyes widened in a different gaze that tries to slip past my face but in this mirror is forever skidding off the surface, bouncing back at myself, my face. I felt giddy and shuddered a bit when I felt the landlady's hand on my shoulder and saw her drunken face with its tousled hair behind me in the mirror.

"Make yourself pretty, my little turtledove," she whispered, "make yourself pretty for love, but don't go on letting him make you pregnant. That's the right one, child, isn't it, this shade?" I stepped back from the mirror, screwed the lipstick back into its case, and said: "Yes, that's the right shade. But I don't have any money."

"Oh never mind, that can wait—later'll do."

"Yes, later," I said. I was still looking into the mirror, skidding around in it as if on ice; covered my eyes with my hand, and finally stepped back.

She piled up some empty soap boxes onto my out-stretched arm, put the lipstick into my apron pocket, and held open the door for me.

"Thanks a lot," I said, "good-bye."

"Good-bye," she said.

I don't understand how Fred can get so furious about the noise the children make. They're so quiet. When I stand by the stove or at the table, they're often so quiet that I suddenly turn around in a panic to make sure they're still there. They build houses out of cartons, whisper together, and when I turn around the fear in my eyes startles them and makes them ask: "What is it, Mother? What is it?"

"Nothing," I say then, "nothing." And I turn away to roll out my dough. I am afraid to leave them alone. I used to be away for an afternoon only, with Fred, only once before for a whole night. The baby is asleep, and I want to try to get away before he wakes up.

Next door the horrible moaning, the cooing and frightful panting that accompany their lovemaking, has ceased. Now they are sleeping before going to a movie. I am beginning to realize that we must buy a radio to drown out this moaning, for the unnaturally loud conversations that I start as soon as that ghastly business begins—that fills me not with disgust, only with horror—those unnatural conversations have a way of quickly petering out, and I ask myself whether the children aren't beginning to catch on. At any rate, they can hear it, and their expressions resemble those of trembling animals sensing death. If at all possible, I try to send them out onto the street, but these early

Sunday afternoons are filled with a melancholy that upsets even the children. My cheeks start to burn the minute that weird, paralyzing silence breaks out, and I try to sing when the first sounds indicate that the struggle has started: the sporadic thumping of the bed, and the cries like those uttered by acrobats as they swing under the big top and change trapezes in midair.

But my voice cracks, and I search in vain for the tunes I have in my head but cannot reproduce. Minutes pass, endless minutes in the leaden melancholy of the Sunday afternoon, and I hear the gasps of exhaustion, hear them light cigarettes, and the ensuing silence is filled with loathing. I slap the dough onto the table, roll it back and forth making as much noise as I can, slap it again, and think of the millions of generations of the poor who have lived without ever having room to make love—and I roll out the dough, turn up the edges, and press the fruit into the pastry.

7

The room was dark, situated at the end of a long corridor, and when I looked out of the window my eyes fell on a dingy brick wall that may at one time have been red, decorated with a brown design, originally yellow, of bricks in Greek-key pattern; and looking past the wall, which stood obliquely to my field of vision, my eyes fell on the two station platforms, now empty. A woman was sitting there on a bench with a child, and the girl from the soft-drink kiosk stood outside the door fidgeting with her white apron, rolling it up and down her thighs. Beyond the station was the cathedral, bedecked with flags, and I felt oppressed by the sight beyond the empty station of people crowding around the altar. I was oppressed by the silence of the crowd outside the cathedral. Then I saw the Bishop in his red robe standing near the altar, and the moment I saw him I heard his voice issuing loud and clear from the loudspeakers across the empty station.

I have often heard the Bishop and have always been bored by his sermons—and I know nothing worse than boredom—but now, on hearing the Bishop's voice coming out of the loudspeaker, I suddenly hit upon the adjective I had been searching for all this time. I had known it was a simple adjective, it had been on the tip of my tongue but had always slipped off. The Bishop loves to employ that shading of dialect that makes a voice popular, but the Bishop's isn't popular. The vocabulary of his sermons always seems to have been taken from lists of theological key words that for the past forty years have been imperceptibly but steadily losing their credibility, words that have become clichés, half-truths. The truth is not boring, but the Bishop apparently has the gift of making it seem so.

... take the Lord our God into our daily lives—build him a tower in our hearts ...

I listened for a few minutes to this voice coming across the deserted platform, at the same time seeing the red-robed figure standing over there by the loudspeaker, speaking in a voice that exaggerated the dialect by the merest nuance, and suddenly the word came to me, the word I had so long been searching for but that was too simple to have occurred to me: the Bishop was stupid. My gaze wandered back over the station where the girl was still fidgeting with her white apron and the woman on the bench was now feeding her baby from a bottle. My gaze wandered over the brownish Greek-key design on the brick wall, crossed the grimy windowsill back into my room, and I closed the window, lay down on the bed, and smoked.

Now I could hear nothing more, and there was not a sound in the building. The walls of my room were papered in a reddish shade, but the green, heart-shaped pattern had faded and merely covered the wallpaper like a washed-out pencil scrawl of unexpected regularity. The light fixture was hideous, like all light fixtures, an egg-shaped glass pouch with blue marbling and probably containing a fifteen-watt bulb. The narrow clothes closet, stained brown, was obviously never used nor ever intended to be. The people who occupy this room are not the kind who unpack their bags—if they have any, that is. They have no jackets to hang on clothes hangers, no shirts to put away in piles, and the two hangers that I could see in the open closet were so flimsy that the weight of my jacket would have been enough to break them. Here you hang your jacket over the back of the chair, throw your trousers on top without bothering to fold them—if you take them off at all, that is—and look down at the pale or perhaps red-cheeked female whose clothese are strewn over the other chair. The closet is superfluous, its existence merely symbolic, like the hangers that no one has ever used. The washstand was nothing more than an ordinary kitchen table with a washbasin sunk into it. But this washbasin was not sunk in. It was enamel, chipped in places, and the soap dish was cheap china, advertising a sponge factory. The tooth glass must have been broken and not replaced. Anyway, there was none. Evidently someone had felt obliged to provide pictures for the walls, and what could be more appropriate than a print of the Mona Lisa that looked as if it had once been the supplement to a popular art magazine? The beds were fairly new, they still had the pungent smell of newly planed wood, and were low and dark. The bed linen did not interest me. For the time being I lay on top, fully dressed, waiting for my wife, who was probably bringing our own linen. The blankets were woolen, grayish green, rather worn, and the pattern in them—of bears playing ball— had turned into people playing ball, for the bears' faces were no longer recognizable, and they now resembled caricatures of bull-necked athletes throwing soap bubbles back and forth. The bells struck twelve.

I got up to fetch the soap dish from the washstand and began to smoke. It seemed terrible that I couldn't talk to anyone about it, couldn't explain the true situation to anyone, but I needed the money, needed the room, merely to sleep with my wife. For the past two months, though we live in the same city, we have had marital relations only in hotel rooms. Sometimes, when the weather was really warm, outdoors in parks or in the hallways of ruined buildings, in the very heart of town where we could be safe from discovery. Our apartment is too small, that's all. Besides, the wall separating us from our neighbors is too thin. For a larger apartment you need money, you need what is known as energy, but we have neither money or energy. Even my wife has no energy.

The last time we lay together was in a park out in the suburbs. It was evening—from the fields came the smell of a harvest of leeks, and on the horizon the chimneys were belching black smoke into the reddish sky. Darkness fell quickly, the red sky turned purple, then black, and we could no longer see the bold brushstroke of the smoking chimneys. The smell of leeks became stronger, mixed with oniony bitterness. A long way off, beyond the hollow of a sandpit, lights were burning, and close to us, along the pathway, a man rode by on a bicycle: the beam of light wavered along the bumpy road cutting a small dark triangle out of the sky, with one side left open. There was a rattle of loose screws, and the clatter of the mudguard died away with an almost ritual sound. If I kept looking I could also see, farther along the path, a wall that was darker than the night sky, and from behind the wall came the cackling of geese and the subdued voice of a woman calling them to be fed.

All I could see of Käte on the dark earth was her white face and the strangely blue shimmer of her eyes when she opened them. Her arms were also white and bare, and she wept bitterly, and when I kissed her I could taste her tears. I felt dizzy, the dome of the sky swayed gently back and forth, and Käte wept more bitterly than ever.

We brushed the dirt from our clothes and slowly walked to the terminus of the Number 9. From a distance we heard the streetcar rounding the loop, saw the sparks from the overhead wire.

"It's getting chilly," said Käte.

"Yes," I said.

"Where are you going to sleep tonight?"

"At the Blocks'."

We walked down the battle-scarred avenue leading to the streetcar.

We sat down in the tavern near the Number 9 terminus; I ordered a brandy for each of us, dropped a coin into the pinball machine, watched the nickel balls bounce into the wooden trough, and flipped them out one by one; they rolled around steel springs, banged into metal contacts, setting off a soft pinging while red, green, and blue scores flashed up on the back glass. The proprietress and Käte were watching me, and as I went on playing I laid my hand on Käte's hair. The proprietress had crossed her arms, her heavy face was lit up by a smile. I went on playing, and Käte watched. A man came into the tavern, slid onto a barstool, put his briefcase behind him on a table, and ordered a schnapps. The man's face was smudged, his hands were brown, and the light blue of his eyes looked lighter than it was. He glanced at my hand, which was still lying on Käte's hair, then at me, and ordered another schnapps. Shortly after that, he stood beside me and played the other machine, which looked quite primitive, almost like a cash register: a crank, a slot, and a reddish panel showing three large black numbers in a row. The man put in a coin, pulled the lever, the numbers at the top revolved, blurred, then—at intervals—came three clicks, the numbers 1 4 6 showed up on the panel.

"Nothing," said the man and dropped in another coin. The disc with the numbers raced around, clunk it went, clunk, and again clunk—there was a moment's silence, and suddenly coins came tumbling out of the muzzle of the machine.

"Four," said the man, and he smiled at me and said: "That's better."

Käte took my hand from her hair and said:
"I have to go."

Outside the streetcar rounded the curve, screeching around the loop, and I paid for the two brandies and took Käte to the streetcar stop. I kissed her as she got on, and she put her hand on my cheek, and waved for as long as I could see her.

When I got back to the tavern, the man with the blackened face was still standing beside the lever. I ordered a brandy, lit a cigarette, and watched him. I thought I could recognize the rhythm when the discs started rotating, felt alarmed when the clicking stop came sooner than seemed right to me, and I could hear the man murmuring: Nothing—nothing—two—nothing—nothing—nothing."

The proprietress's pale face was unsmiling now when the man left the tavern with a curse, and I got some change so I could start pulling the lever. I'll never forget the moment when first I pressed down the lever that made the discs rotate at what seemed to me a fantastic speed—and how there were three clicks at varying intervals, and I listened for the jingle of tumbling coins: nothing came out.

I stayed on there for almost half an hour, drinking schnapps, and working the lever, listening to the frenzied spinning of the discs and the dry clicking; and when I left the tavern I hadn't a penny in my pocket and had to walk all the way to Escher Street, where the Blocks live, almost three quarters of an hour.

Since then I have been going only to those taverns

that have this kind of machine; I listen to the fascinating rhythm of the discs, wait for the clicks, and get a shock every time the discs stop and nothing comes out.

Our meetings are subject to a rhythm that we have not yet explored. Suddenness governs the tempo, and it can happen that in the evening, before I start looking for a place to spend the night, I often go to our building and get Käte to come downstairs by ringing the bell in a prearranged way so the children won't know I'm around. For the strange thing is that they seem to love me, to miss me, to talk about me, although I used to smack them during the last few weeks I was still with them: I struck them so hard that I was shocked by the look on my face when I caught sight of myself in the mirror, hair disheveled, pale yet bathed in sweat, my hands covering my ears so as not to hear the screams of the boy I had beaten because he had been singing. On one occasion they discovered me, Clemens and Carla, one Saturday afternoon as I was waiting downstairs in the entrance for Käte. I was startled to see their faces light up at the sight of me. They rushed toward me, hugged me, asked whether I was well, and I went upstairs with them. But as soon as I entered our room I was seized with horror again—the ghastly breath of poverty—even the smile of our baby, who seemed to recognize me, the pleasure of my wife: nothing had the power to suppress that hateful irritation that mounted in me as soon as the children began to dance around and sing. I left them before my irritation got the better of me.

But often, as I'm sitting in a bar, their faces suddenly well up among the beer glasses and bottles in front of me, and I still can't get over the shock of seeing my children this morning in the procession.

I jumped up from the bed at the first notes of the closing hymn outside the cathedral, I opened the window and saw the red figure of the Bishop walking through the crowd.

In the window below me I saw the black hair of a woman whose dress was covered with dandruff. Her head seemed to be lying on the windowsill. Suddenly she turned to me, it was the thin, greasy face of the landlady.

"If you want to eat," she called up, "you'd better hurry."

"Yes," I said, "I'm coming."

As I was walking down the stairs, the cannonade of the toothpaste company started up again on the embankment.

8

The cake had turned out well. As I took it out of the oven, the warm, sweet smell of baking flowed into our room. The children were all smiles. I sent Clemens for some cream, filled a pastry tube, and to please the children squirted curlicues and circles, little raised designs, on the plum-blue surface. I watched them scraping the remains of the cream out of the bowl and was pleased to see how scrupulously Clemens doled it out. When a spoonful was left over, he gave it to the baby who sat in his high chair and smiled at me as I washed my hands and put on the new lipstick.

"Will you be gone long?"

"Yes, till tomorrow morning."

"Is Father coming back soon?"

"Yes."

Blouse and skirt hung on the side of the kitchen cupboard. I changed in the cubicle and heard the young man arrive who is going to look after the children: he charges only one mark an hour, but from four in the afternoon till seven in the morning, that's fifteen hours, fifteen marks, and it is understood that he gets his meals and, in the evening, when his real duties start, finds cigarettes beside the radio. The radio has been lent me by the Hopfs.

Bellermann seems to be fond of the children, at any rate they like him, and whenever I have been away they tell me about the games he played with them, the stories he told them. He was recommended to me by the chaplain, he has obviously been told about the reasons for my leaving the children, and invariably frowns slightly at the sight of my made-up mouth.

I put on my blouse, fixed up my hair, and went into the room. Bellermann had brought along a girl, a gentle blonde who was already holding the baby in her arms, spinning his rattle around her finger, which he seemed to find amusing. Bellermann introduced the girl to me, but I didn't catch her name. Her smile, her extraordinary tenderness toward the baby, had something of the professional about it, and her eyes told me that she considers me unfit to be a mother.

Bellermann has kinky black hair, a pale, greasy complexion, and his nose is always wrinkled.

"May we go out with the children?" the girl asked, and I saw Clemens' pleading eyes, saw Carla's nod, and I consented. I looked in the drawer for some money for chocolate, but the girl refused it.

"Please," she said, 'if you don't mind I'd like to pay for the chocolate myself."

"Of course," I said, put the money back in the drawer, and felt miserable beside this radiant specimen of young womanhood.

"You can trust Gulli," said Bellermann, "she's crazy about kids."

I looked at each of my children in turn: Clemens, Carla, the baby, and felt my eyes filling with tears. Clemens nodded to me and said: "It's all right, Mother, nothing's going to happen. We won't go near the water."

"Please," I said to the girl, "don't go near the water."

"No, of course not!" said Bellermann, and they both laughed.

Bellermann helped me on with my coat, I picked up my bag, kissed the children, and blessed them. I felt superfluous.

I paused a moment outside the door, heard them laughing inside, and slowly walked down the stairs.

It was only half-past three, and the streets were still empty. Some children were playing hopscotch. They looked up as my footsteps approached. All was quiet in this street, where many hundreds of people live, except for my footsteps. From far down the street came the faint tinkling of a piano, and behind a curtain that barely moved I saw an old woman with a sallow face holding a fat mongrel in her arms. Even though we have been living here for eight years, I invariably feel dizzy when I look up: the gray walls, patchily repaired, seem to lean forward, and up and down the narrow gray street of the sky ran the thin tinkling of the piano, the sounds imprisoned, the melody fragmented that a girl's pale finger sought and did not find. I walked faster, hurrying past the children whose eyes seemed to hold a threat for me.

Fred ought not to leave me alone. Although I am looking forward to meeting him, it upsets me to have to leave the children in order to be with him. Whenever I ask him where he is living, he is evasive, and those Blocks where he says he has been staying for the past month are people I don't know, and he won't tell me the address. Sometimes in the evening we meet in a café for a brief half hour while our landlady keeps an eye on the children. We embrace hurriedly at a streetcar stop, and when I get on the streetcar Fred stands there and waves. There are nights when I lie on our sofa and cry, while all around me there is silence. I hear the children breathing, the baby stirring restlessly because he is teething, and as I weep I pray and listen to the hollow grinding sound of time running out around me. I was twenty-three when we got married—since then fifteen years have passed, rolled away without my noticing, but I need only see the faces of my children to know that each year added to their lives is taken away from my own.

At Tuckhoff Square I got on a bus and looked into the silent streets, where only here and there a few people were standing at a cigarette kiosk. I got off at Benekam Street and entered the porch of the Church of the Seven Sorrows to find out when there would be an evening Mass.

It was dark in the porch, I looked in my bag for matches, groping among loose cigarettes, lipstick, handkerchief, and toilet articles, finally found the box and struck a match. I jumped: over to the right someone was standing in a dark niche, someone who did not

move. I tried to call out something that sounded like
"Hello," but my voice had shrunk with fear and the
pounding of my heart interfered. The figure did not
budge, it held something in its hands that looked like
a stick. I threw away the burnt match, struck a new
one, and even when I realized that it was a statue my
heart didn't stop pounding. I took a step nearer, and
in the faint light I recognized a stone angel with flowing
curls, holding a lily in one hand. I bent forward till my
chin almost touched the figure's breast, and looked for
a long time into the face of the angel. Face and hair
were covered with a thick layer of dust, and even the
blind eye sockets were filled with black flakes. I carefully blew them away, freeing the entire gentle oval
from dust, and suddenly I saw that the smile was made
of plaster, and that together with the dust the magic of
the smile was blown away too; yet I kept on, blew the
dust off those splendid curls, the breast, the flowing
robe, and carefully pursing my lips cleaned the lily—
my pleasure dwindled the more the crude colors became visible, the heartless paint of the devotional trade,
and I turned slowly away, advancing farther into the
porch, to look for the notices. Once again I struck a
match, saw in the background the dim red of the
perpetual lamp, and was startled as I stood before the
black bulletin board: this time someone really was coming up to me from behind. I turned and sighed with
relief on recognizing the pale round peasant's face of a
priest. He stopped in front of me, his eyes looked sad.
My match went out, and he asked me in the dark:

"Are you looking for something?"

"A Mass," I said, "where is there a Mass in the evening?"

"Holy Mass," he said, "in the cathedral at five."

I saw only his hair, blond, lusterless, his eyes that gleamed dully, I heard the streetcar rounding the corner outside, heard cars honking, and said suddenly into the darkness:

"I'd like to confess." I was shocked at myself but also felt relieved, and the priest said, as if he had been waiting for this:

"Come with me."

"No, here please," I said.

"That won't do," he said gently. "In fifteen minutes, the service will be beginning, and people might come. The confessional is inside." I had felt an impulse, in this dark, drafty porch, close to the plaster angel, the distant perpetual lamp in view, to tell the priest everything, to whisper it into his ear in the darkness and to receive the whispered absolution.

Instead I followed him obediently into the courtyard, and the uncontrollable enthusiasm that for a moment had gripped me fell away as we walked between fallen masonry and fragments of sandstone from the church wall toward the little gray house that stands close to the wall of the streetcar depot from where the sound of hammering on metal penetrated the Sunday afternoon. When the door opened, I looked into the coarse, amazed face of the housekeeper, who eyed me suspiciously.

It was dark in the hall, and the priest said to me:

"Wait a moment, please."

From somewhere or other, around a corner I could

not see, came the clattering of dishes, and all of a sudden I recognized the disagreeable, sickly smell clinging to the hall, evidently well entrenched in the damp burlap covering the wall: the warm steam of turnip tops came wafting from the corner beyond which the kitchen must be. At last, light came from a door in the hall, and I could make out the shadow of the priest in the pale beam. "Over here," he called.

I approached uncertainly. The room looked dreadful: behind a red curtain in the corner there seemed to be a bed, I thought I could smell it. Bookshelves of varying sizes, some crooked, were set up against the wall, and around a huge table stood a random group of valuable antique chairs upholstered in black velvet. On the table were books, a package of tobacco, cigarette papers, a bag of carrots, and an assortment of newspapers. The priest stood behind the table, beckoned me forward while pushing toward me a chair with a grille nailed to one arm, at right angles to the table. I liked his face, now that I could see all of him in the light.

"I must apologize," he said, with a glance toward the door and a slight nod of his head. "We're country people, and I can't persuade her not to pickle turnip tops. It's much more expensive than buying them ready cooked, if I count the fuel, the dirt, the smell, and the work—but I can't make her see it—do sit down." He moved the chair with the grille close to the table, sat down on it, and beckoned me. I walked around the table and sat down beside him, facing him through the grille.

The priest placed the stole around his shoulders,

leaned his arms on the table, and the way he hid his
profile with his cupped hand seemed somehow studied
and professional. Some of the squares in the grille were
broken, and when I started to whisper: "In the name of
the Father, the Son, and the Holy Ghost . . ." he looked
at his wristwatch, I followed his glance and saw that it
was three minutes past four. I began to speak, I whispered all my fear, all my pain, all my life into his ear,
my fear of desire, fear of receiving Holy Communion,
the turbulence of our marriage. I told him my husband
had left me, that I met him only now and then in order
to lie with him—and when I hesitated for a few seconds
he shot a glance at his watch, and each time I followed
his glance and saw how slowly the hand was moving
forward. Then he raised his lids, I saw his eyes, the
yellow nicotine stains on his fingers, and he lowered his
eyes again and said: "Go on." He said it gently, yet it
hurt me, the way it hurts when a skilled hand presses
the pus out of a wound.

And I went on whispering in his ear, told him everything about the time two years ago when we were both
drinking, Fred and I—about the death of my children,
about the living children, about what we have to listen
to from the Hopfs' room next door and what the
Hopfs heard from ours. And I hesitated again. And
again he looked at his watch, again I looked at it too
and saw that it was only six minutes past four. And
again he raised his eyelids, said gently: "Go on," and I
whispered faster, told him about my hatred for the
priests who live in big houses and have faces like ad-
vertisements for face cream—about Mrs. Franke, our

powerlessness, our dirt, and finally I told him that I was probably pregnant again.

And when I paused again he did not look at his watch, he raised his lids for half a second longer, asked me: "Is that all?" And I said "Yes" and looked at his watch, which was right before my eyes since he had taken his hands from his face and clasped them on the edge of the table: it was eleven minutes past four, and involuntarily I looked into the depths of his loose sleeve, saw his hairy, muscular peasant's arm, the rolled-up shirt sleeve, and thought: Why doesn't he roll down his sleeves?

He sighed, placed his hands over his face again, and murmured: "Do you pray?" and I said: "Yes," told him that sometimes I lie there all night on my shabby sofa reciting all the prayers I can remember, that often I light a candle so as not to wake the children, and read from the prayerbook those prayers I don't know by heart.

He asked no more questions, I was silent too and looked at the watch on his wrist: it was fourteen minutes past four, and outside I could hear the hammering in the streetcar depot, the tralala-ing of the housekeeper in the kitchen, the rumbling of a train in the station.

At last he took his hands from his face, folded them over his knees, and said without looking at me: " 'In the world ye shall have tribulation: but be of good cheer; I have overcome the world.' Do you realize what that means?" And without waiting for my reply he went on: " 'Enter ye in at the strait gate: for wide is the gate, and broad is the way that leadeth to destruction, and many there be which go in thereat; because strait is the gate, and narrow is the way, which leadeth unto life, and few there be that find it.' "

He fell silent again, placed his hands over his face again, and murmured from between his fingers: "Narrow—the narrowest way we know is along a knife edge, and you seem to me to be walking along it . . . ," and suddenly he removed his hands, looked at me through the gap in the grille, for barely a second, and I was startled by the severity in his eyes, which had seemed so kindly. "I order you," he said, "I order you to hear the Holy Mass of your priest whom you hate so much, to receive Holy Communion from his hands —when," he looked at me again, "when you have received absolution."

He fell silent again, seemed to be brooding, and while in my mind I tried to utter all the prayers, all the sighs, I know, I could hear the hissing of welding torches outside in the depot and suddenly the pealing of his church bells. It was a quarter past four.

"I don't know whether I can absolve you, we must wait. In God's name," he said abruptly, and now his eyes had lost their severity—"how can you harbor so much hatred?" He made a gesture of helplessness, turned toward me: "I can bless you—but you'll have to forgive me, I have to give it some more thought, perhaps discuss it with a brother priest. Can you come back this evening—oh no, you're meeting your husband. You must see to it that your husband returns to you."

I was very distressed that he would not absolve me,

and I said: "Please absolve me." He smiled, raised his hand slightly, and said: "I wish I could because you yearn for it so much, but I really have doubts. Do you feel no more hatred?"

"No, no," I said hastily, "it just makes me sad."

He seemed to hesitate, and I didn't know what to do. If I had persisted, he might have done it, but I wanted to be genuinely absolved and not because of my persuasion.

"Conditionally," he said and smiled again. "I can absolve you conditionally—I have such doubts—but on condition that I actually do have the authority I might . . . ," he waved his hands impatiently in front of my face—"with your hatred you are judging—but we mustn't judge, mustn't hate. No." He shook his head vigorously, then held his face in his cupped hands on the edge of the table, prayed, got up suddenly, and absolved me. I crossed myself and stood up.

He stood beside the table, his eyes on me, and I suddenly felt sorry for him, even before he began to speak.

"I can only—" he swept away the words with a gesture. "Do you think I don't feel it, this hatred, I a priest? I feel it here"—he tapped his black cassock just below his heart—"this hatred for my superiors, sometimes. Here," he said, pointing toward the window, "in my church Masses are said by visiting priests, they come from the nearby hotels, well-groomed men on their way to a conference, coming from a conference, grumbling about the dirt, the lack of Mass-servers—the ten-minute Masses, the thirteen-, twenty-, and standard twenty-five-minute ones, are said here. Five, ten, often fifteen a day. You have no idea how many priests are traveling around, they are returning from health resorts, on their way there—and conferences, there are plenty of those. Fifteen Masses with less than five worshipers taking part in the whole lot. Here," he said, "is where all records are broken, the odds are fifteen to five—but then, why should I hate them, those poor priests who leave the perfume of luxury hotel bathrooms behind in my run-down old sacristy?"

He turned from the window to face me again, handed me a pad and pencil from the table, I wrote down my address and straightened my hat.

There were several loud knocks at the door.

"I know, I know," he called. "The service, I'm coming!"

He shook hands with me as we parted, looked at me with a sigh, and showed me to the door.

I walked slowly past the church porch toward the underpass. Two women and a man were going to the service in the church, across from the church hung a big white banner that said in red letters:

WHERE WOULD YOU BE WITHOUT YOUR DRUGGIST?

Up in the sky the edge of a dark cloud slid past the sun, uncovering it, and now the sun was entirely suspended in the big D of DRUGGIST, filling it with yellow light. I walked on. A small boy passed me, with a prayerbook under his arm, then the street was empty. It was lined by shacks and rubble, and behind the charred façades I could hear the noises from the depot.

I stopped at the sudden warm smell of fresh baking, looked to the right, into the open door of a wooden

shack from which coils of white steam were escaping:
on the threshold a child was sitting in the sun, squint-
ing up into the sky, the mild expression of idiocy, the
red-rimmed eyelids that looked transparent in the sunlight—I felt a pang of tenderness: the child was holding
a fresh doughnut in his hand, his mouth was all smeared
with sugar, and now when he bit into the doughnut
brownish jam oozed out and dripped onto his sweater.
Inside, bending over a saucepan, was a young girl: she
had a lovely face, a skin of paper-thin delicacy, and
although her hair was covered by a scarf I saw she
must be a blonde. She was fishing hot doughnuts out of
the steaming fat, placing them on a grill, and suddenly
she looked up, our eyes met, and she smiled at me. Her
smile had a magical effect on me, I smiled back, and we
remained thus for several seconds, without moving,
and while I actually saw only her—I saw, as from a
great distance, myself as well, saw the two of us standing there, smiling at each other like sisters, and I lowered my gaze when I remembered that I had no money
to buy one of her doughnuts, the smell of which was
stirring up my stomach. I look down at the idiot's tow-
head, wished I had brought along some money. I never
do when I am meeting Fred because he can't resist the
sight of money and usually persuades me to spend it
on drink. I saw the idiot's thick neck, the sugary crumbs
spread all over his face, and something like envy rose
in me as I regarded his slightly parted lips.

When I raised my eyes again the girl had pushed the
saucepan aside and was just undoing her head scarf;
she took it off and her hair tumbled into the sunshine:

and once again I saw not only her, saw myself as well, as from a great height, the street, dirty, flanked with ruins, the porch of the church, the banner, and myself standing at the entrance of this shack: skinny and sad, but smiling.

I walked carefully past the idiot into the shack. In the corner two children were sitting at a table, and beside the stove an old man, unshaven, was reading the paper. He lowered the pages and looked at me.

The girl was standing beside the coffee machine, she looked into the mirror and patted her hair; I observed her very small, white, childlike hands, and now saw in the mirror, beside her fresh young face that was smiling at me, my own—thin, rather sallow, with the narrow upswept wings of the crimson, made-up mouth: the smile on my face, though coming from within me, almost against my will, seemed false, and now our heads suddenly seemed to switch places, she had my head, I had hers—and I saw myself as a young girl standing in front of the mirror, patting my hair— saw her, that child, spread open at night to a man whom she would love, who would inject life and death into her, leaving behind on her face the traces of what he called love, until it would resemble my own face: thin and sallowed by the bitterness of this life.

But now she turned around, concealing my face in the mirror, and I stepped to the right, surrendering to her charm.

"Good afternoon," I said.

"Good afternoon," she said. "Would you like some doughnuts?"

"No thank you," I said.

"Why not, don't they smell good?"

"They do," I said, and trembled at the thought of the unknown man to whom she would give herself. "They really do—but I didn't bring any money."

At the word "money" the old man beside the stove stood up, came behind the counter, stood beside the girl, and said: "Money? But you can pay later. You'd like some doughnuts, wouldn't you?"

"Yes," I said.

"Oh, do sit down," said the girl.

I walked back a few steps and sat down at the table beside the children.

"Coffee too?" called the girl.

"Yes please," I said.

The old man piled three doughnuts onto a plate and brought them over to me. He waited beside me.

"Thank you very much," I said, "but you don't know me."

He smiled at me, took his hands from behind his back, held them awkwardly over his stomach, and murmured: "Oh, don't worry." I nodded toward the idiot, who was sitting on the threshold: "Is that your son?"

"My son," he said softly, "and that's my daughter." He glanced at the girl behind the counter who was working the levers of the coffee machine.

"He doesn't understand the language of humans, my son doesn't," said the old man, "nor that of animals, he can't say a single word, only *dzu-dza-dzay*, and we"— his tongue, which he had raised to form those sounds, flattened itself in his mouth again—"we imitate him, awkwardly, harshly, we say *tzu-tza-tzay*. We're incapable," he said softly, and suddenly he raised his voice a little, called "Bernhard," and the idiot clumsily turned his head but immediately let it fall forward again. Once again the old man called "Bernhard," again the child turned, his head flopped forward again like a pendulum, and the old man got up, took the child carefully by the hand, and led him to the table. He sat down beside me on the chair, lifted the boy onto his lap, and asked me gently:

"Or does he upset you? Just say so."

"No," I said, "he doesn't." His daughter brought the coffee, set the cup in front of me, and stood beside her father. "You must say if he disgusts you, we won't mind, most people feel disgusted."

The child was fat, smeared all over, his gaze blank, babbling his *dzu-dza-dzay*. I had a good look at him, raised my head again, and said: "No, he doesn't disgust me—he's like a baby." I raised the cup to my lips, drank some coffee, took a bite of the doughnut, and said: "My, your coffee's good!"

"Really?" the girl exclaimed, "really? A man told me that this morning—no one else ever has."

"It really is good," I said, and drank some more, took another bite of the doughnut. The girl leaned on the back of her father's chair, looked at me, then beyond me.

"Sometimes," she said, "I try to imagine how he experiences things, how he lives—he is usually so peaceful, so happy—maybe to him air is water, green water, because he finds it so difficult to move through it—green water that sometimes changes to brown, interspersed with black streaks like in an old movie—sometimes he cries too, that's terrible, when there are certain noises, the screeching of streetcars, the piercing whistle in the radio—when that happens, he cries."

"Oh," I said, "he cries?"

"Oh yes," she said, and she brought her gaze back, looking at me without smiling. "He often cries, and always at those shrill sounds. He cries hard then, and the tears run down into the mess around his mouth. It's the only thing he likes to eat: sweet stuff, milk, and bread—anything that's not sweet, not milk or bread—he brings it all up again. Oh, I'm sorry," she said, "now you're disgusted."

"No," I said. "Tell me about him."

She looked beyond me again, put her hand on the idiot's head. "Just as it's difficult for him to move his face, his body, against the flow of the air—it must be just as terrible for him to hear those sounds. Maybe his ear is always full of the gentle throbbing of organs, a brown melody that he alone can hear—maybe he hears a storm rustling the leaves of invisible trees. Violin strings as thick as arms resound—a buzz that calls him, that is destroyed."

The old man listened to her spellbound, holding his hands clasped around the body of the idiot and ignoring the jam and sugar dribbling onto his sleeves. I drank some more coffee, took a bite of the second doughnut, and asked the girl softly: "How do you know?" She looked at me, smiled, and said: "Oh, I don't know anything—but perhaps—there must be something in him that we don't know, I try to imagine it—sometimes, too, he cries out suddenly, quite suddenly, comes running to me, and I let his tears flow into my apron—quite suddenly, while he's sitting at the door—and I imagine that then, in a flash, he sees everything the way we see it—suddenly—for only half a second—that it pierces him like a stab of terror: people, the way we see them, cars, trains—all the noises. Then he cries for a long time."

The children who had been sitting in the corner got up, pushed away their plates, walked past us, and a pert little girl in a green beret called out: "Charge it, please —my mother says."

"Yes, that's all right," said the old man and smiled after them.

"Your wife," I asked gently, "his mother is dead?"

"Yes," said the man, "she's dead—a bomb blew her to pieces on the street, tore the baby from her arms, he landed on a bale of straw and was found screaming."

"Was he, I mean, from birth . . . ?" I asked.

"From birth," said the girl. "He was always like that, everything trickles, trickles past him—only our voices reach him, organs in church, the screech of the street-car, and the chanting of the monks. But why aren't you eating—oh, but you *are* disgusted."

I picked up the last doughnut, shook my head, and asked: "He can hear the monks, you say?"

"Yes," she said gently, her eyes on me. "He must be able to hear them. When I go to hear the monks, on Bildoner Square, you know—when they do their chanting there—then his face changes, gets narrow, looks almost severe—I get a shock every time—and he listens, I know he can hear them, he listens, he becomes quite different, he hears the melody of the prayers, and he cries when the monks stop. You're surprised!" she said with a smile. "Do go on eating!"

I picked up the doughnut again, took a mouthful, felt the warm jam melting in my mouth.

"You must go there with him quite often," I said, "to Bildoner Square."

"Oh yes," she said, "I often go there with him, although it's always such a shock. Would you like some more coffee?"

"No, thank you," I said, "I have to go." I looked at her hesitantly, also at the idiot, and said: "I'd like to see it one day."

"In the church?" she asked, "with the monks?"

"Yes," I said.

"Oh, why don't you come along—what a pity you're leaving—you'll be back, won't you?"

"I'll be back," I said. "I still have to pay my bill."

"Not for that reason, please—do come back." The old man nodded at her words. I finished my coffee, stood up, and brushed the crumbs off my coat.

"I'll be back," I said, "it's so nice here."

"Today?" asked the girl.

"Not today," I said, "but soon, maybe tomorrow morning—and often—and I'll go with you to hear the monks."

"Yes," she said. She gave me her hand, I held on to it for a moment, that very slender, white hand, I looked into her fresh young face, smiled, and nodded to the old man. "Bernhard," I said softly to the idiot, who was crumbling the doughnut between his fingers, but he did not hear me, did not even seem to see me—he had almost entirely closed his lids, those red-rimmed, inflamed eyelids.

I turned away and walked toward the dark underpass leading into Station Street.

9

When I came downstairs, plates were being carried away in stacks from the tables, there was a smell of cold goulash, salad, artificially sweetened pudding. I sat down in a corner and watched two youths playing the machines. The high-pitched pinging produced by the nickel balls touching the contacts, the whirling of the discs in the slot machine, and the clinking stops, excited me. The waiter brushed off the tables with his napkin, and the thin landlady tacked a large yellow cardboard sign over the counter: DANCING TONIGHT. ADMISSION FREE.

At the table next to me sat an old man in a loden coat and a green felt hat, his pipe smouldering in the ashtray. The man had kept on his green hat and was poking around in the paprika goulash.

"What would you like?" asked the waiter. I looked up at him, and his face seemed familiar.

"What have you got?"

"Goulash," he said, "pork chops, potatoes, salad, pudding—and soup to start, if you like."

"I'll have the goulash," I said, "and soup to start, and a schnapps."

"Right away, sir," said the waiter.

The food was hot and hearty, and I realized I was hungry, asked for some bread, and sopped up the peppery gravy.

I ordered another schnapps. The youths were still at it. The hair of one of them stuck up from his part.

I paid, waited a few more minutes, but the machines were still occupied. Once again I looked closely at the waiter's face: that pale face, that fair, almost white, hair —I must have seen them somewhere.

When I asked at the counter for some cigarettes, the landlady looked at me and asked: "Are you staying the whole night?"

"Yes," I said.

"Would you mind paying in advance, it's just—" she grinned—"that we feel safer that way, so close to the station, and you've no luggage."

"Of course," I said, and took out my money. "Eight marks, please," she said, and she licked her indelible pencil to write me out a receipt. "Are you expecting someone?" she asked as she handed me the slip.

"Yes, my wife," I said.

"That's all right," she said, handing me the cigarettes, and I put down a mark and went upstairs.

I lay on the bed for a long time, brooding and smoking, with no idea what I was thinking about until I remembered that I was trying to place the waiter's face. I can't forget a face, they all follow me, and I recognize them as soon as they turn up again. They paddle around in my subconscious, especially those I've only seen once, and very briefly, they swim around like shadowy gray fish among the weeds in a muddy pond. Sometimes their heads thrust up almost to the surface, but they emerge totally when I actually see them again. Restlessly I hunted through the swarm in this pond, jerked up the line, and there he was, the waiter: a soldier who had once lain beside me for a minute at a field hospital; I remembered seeing the lice crawling out of the bandage around his head, they had wallowed in the clotted blood as well as the fresh, lice that had crawled unhindered over his neck into the sparse, almost white hair, over the face of the unconscious man, intrepid creatures climbing up his ears, sliding off, landing on his shoulders and disappearing again into the dirty collar —a narrow, suffering face that I had seen two thousand miles from here—that was now casually serving me goulash.

I was glad when I knew where to place the waiter; I turned over on my side, took my money out of my pocket, and counted it on the pillow: I had sixteen marks and eighty pfennigs left.

Then I went down again into the bar, but the two youths were still standing at the machines. One of them seemed to have one of his outside pockets full of coins, it sagged heavily, his right hand was groping around in the money. The only other person left was the man in the green felt hat, drinking beer and reading the paper. I had a schnapps, my eyes on the poreless face of the landlady, who was sitting on a stool leafing through a magazine.

Once again I went upstairs, lay down on the bed, smoked, and thought about Käte and the children, about the war and the two babies who, the priests assure us, are in heaven. I think about these children every day, but today I thought about them for a very long time, and no one who knows me, not even Käte, would believe how often I think of them. They regard me as an unstable person who changes his job every three years since the money left him by his father has gone down the drain, a person who, even with advancing age, acquires no stability, is indifferent to his family, and drinks whenever he has the money to do so.

But actually I drink very seldom, not even every month, and I hardly get properly drunk once in three months, and I sometimes wonder: What do all those people think I do the days I don't drink—and that's twenty-nine out of thirty. I walk a lot, try to earn some money on the side dredging up some of the things I learned at school and selling them to struggling fifth-graders. I stroll through the city, usually far out into the suburbs, and visit the cemeteries when they are open. I walk around among the well-tended shrubs, the neat flower beds, read the inscriptions, the names, absorb the smell of the cemetery, and feel my heart quiver with the certainty that I, too, will lie there. At one time we used to travel a lot, in the days when we still had money—but in strange cities I did the same things I now do here, where I intend to remain: I lay about on hotel beds, smoked, or went for aimless walks —now and then entering a church or walking far out into the suburbs where the cemeteries are. I drank in cheap taverns, made friends at night with strangers whom I knew I would never see again.

Even as a child, I used to like going to cemeteries, indulging a passion that was not considered suitable for a young person. But all those names, those flower beds, every single letter, the smell—it all tells me that I too will die: the only truth I have never doubted. And sometimes, in those endless rows I slowly wander past, I find names of people I knew.

As a child I already experienced the reality of death. My mother died when I was seven, and I carefully observed everything they did with her: the priest came and annointed her, blessed her—she lay and did not move. Flowers were delivered, a coffin, relatives came, wept, and prayed at her bedside—she lay and did not move. I observed everything with curiosity. Being smacked did not prevent me from watching the men from the funeral home. They washed my mother, dressed her in a white gown, arranged the flowers all around her coffin, they nailed down the lid, loaded the coffin into a car—and the apartment was empty, without my mother. And without telling my father I went to the cemetery, took the Number 12—oh, I'll never forget—transferred at Tuckhoff Square onto a Number 10, and rode as far as the terminus.

It was the first time I had ever been to a cemetery, I asked the man in the green cap at the gate where my mother was. He had a puffy red face, smelled of wine, took me by the hand, and walked across with me to the administration building. He was very kind to me, asked my name, led me into a room, and told me to wait. I waited. I walked about among the chairs, around the light-brown table, looked at the pictures on the wall, and waited: one picture showed a slender, dark woman sitting on an island and waiting, I stood on tiptoe and tried to read what was written underneath, and managed to make out: NANA. Another picture showed a bearded man, grinning and holding a beer mug with a richly ornamented lid up to his face. I couldn't read what was underneath, went to the door—but the door was locked. Then I began to cry, I sat quietly on one of the light-brown chairs and cried until I heard footsteps in the corridor: it was my father approaching: I had so often heard his footsteps approaching through our long corridor. My father was kind to me, and together with the fat man in the green cap who smelled of wine we went across to the morgue, and I saw them standing there, coffins with names and numbers, and the man in the green cap led us to one coffin, and my father tapped the label with his finger and read out to me: Elisabeth Bogner. 18/4, 4 P.M. Plot VII/L. And he asked me what date it was. I didn't know, and he said: "The sixteenth. Mother won't be buried till the day after tomorrow." I wanted to be sure that nothing would happen to the coffin that I wouldn't see, and my father wept, promised me, and I followed him into the gloomy apartment, helped him to clean out the large old-fashioned storeroom, and we unearthed all the things my mother had bought throughout the years from her peddlers: stacks of rusty razor blades, soap, insect powder, perished elastic, and many boxes of safety pins. My father wept.

Two days later I actually did see the coffin again, just as it had been. They loaded it onto a cart, hung wreaths and flowers on it, and we followed the coffin, walking behind the priest, the acolytes, up to the big muddy hole on Plot VII, and I saw the coffin being blessed, lowered, sprinkled with holy water, and scattered with earth. And I listened to the priest's prayer as he spoke of dust, of dust and resurrection.

We stayed behind at the cemetery for a long time, my father and I, because I insisted on watching: the gravediggers threw more earth on top, stamped it down, patted a little mound into shape with their spades, laid the wreaths on it, and finally one of them stuck a small white cross with a black inscription into the earth, and on it I could read: Elisabeth Bogner.

Even as a child I thought I knew exactly what it meant to be dead: one had disappeared, been buried in the ground, and waited for the resurrection. And I understood, noted it carefully: all men must die, and they did, many whom I knew, whose funerals no one could keep me from attending.

Maybe I think too much about death, and those who regard me as a drinker are mistaken. Whatever I try my hand at seems of no consequence, boring, and irrelevant, and since I have left Käte and the children I have begun to go to the cemeteries again, try to be there early enough to take part in funerals; I follow the coffins of unknown dead, listen to the funeral sermons, respond to the liturgy the priest murmurs over the open grave, I throw earth into the holes, pray beside the coffins, and if I have any money I first buy some flowers and scatter them singly onto the loose earth piled on the coffin. I walk past the weeping relatives, and on occasion I have even been invited back to the house. I would sit at table with perfect strangers, drink beer, and eat potato salad and sausage, allow weeping women to pile my plate with huge open-face sandwiches, smoke cigarettes, drink schnapps, and listen to the life history of people of whom I knew nothing but their coffin. They would also show me photos—a week ago I followed the coffin of a young girl and later sat in the corner room of an old-fashioned restaurant beside her father, who took me for a secret admirer of his daughter. He showed me pictures of her, pictures of a really beautiful creature: her hair blowing in the wind, she was sitting on a motor scooter at the entrance to a tree-lined avenue. "She was just a child," her father told me, "knew nothing about love." I had scattered flowers on her coffin, now saw the tears in her father's eyes as he put down his cigar for a moment in the gray earthenware ashtray in order to wipe his eyes.

I cared nothing for all those various occupations that I attempted. I couldn't muster the seriousness required for a proper occupation. Before the war I had worked for a long time in a pharmaceutical wholesale house, until I was seized by boredom and switched to photography, of which I also soon tired. Then I decided to become a librarian, although I don't enjoy reading, and it was in a library that I met Käte, who loves books. I stayed on because Käte was there, but we soon got married, and she had to leave when she became pregnant for the first time. Then the war came too, and our first child, Clemens, was born when I was called up.

I didn't want to think about the war, got up from my bed, and went downstairs again to the bar: it was almost four. I had a schnapps, went to the machines, which were now free, but I only dropped in one coin, pressed the lever, and realized I was tired.

I went back to my room, lay down on the bed again, smoked, thought about Käte, until I heard the bells pealing from the Church of the Seven Sorrows. . . .

10

I had no trouble finding the sign with the painted black hand and followed the pointing finger. The street was gray and empty, and as I walked on a lot of people suddenly came streaming out of a narrow building, and I saw that a movie theater was emptying. At the corner there was another sign with a painted black hand, the finger was bent: I was facing Holland House. I was shocked at how dirty the building was, slowly crossed the street, stopped in front of the cheaply painted red entry, pushed open the door, and walked into the restaurant. Three men were standing at the counter. They looked at me as I went in, their conversation stopped, they looked toward the landlady, and the landlady glanced up from her magazine and looked at me. Her eyes traveled from my face to my hat, then to the bag I was carrying; she leaned forward a little to inspect my shoes and legs, then looked me in the face again, staring for quite a while at my lips as if trying to guess the brand of lipstick. Once again she leaned forward, looked doubtfully at my legs, and slowly asked: "Yes?" She removed her hands from her hips, placed them on the metal counter, then folded them over her stomach, and her thin white face took on a puzzled expression.

"My husband's expecting me," I said, and the men turned away, resumed their conversation, and before I had given my name the landlady said: "Number eleven, second floor." She pointed to the swing door beside the counter. One of the men rushed to the door and held it open for me. He was pale and seemed to be drunk: his lips were trembling, and the whites of his eyes were bloodshot. He lowered his eyes when I looked at him, I said "Thank you," walked through the open door, and as I went up the stairs I could hear through the still swinging door a voice saying: "She's not from out of town."

The stairwell had green walls, beyond the frosted glass panes one could see the shadow of a black wall, and on the second floor, in a small hallway, an unshaded light bulb was burning.

I knocked at the door with the number 11, and when no answer came from inside, I opened it and went in. Fred was lying on the bed, asleep. He looks fragile, almost childlike, lying in bed, and could be mistaken for an eighteen-year-old were it not for his careworn face. When he sleeps his lips are slightly parted, his dark hair falls over his forehead, his face looks as if he were unconscious—he sleeps deeply. Coming up the stairs I had still been angry with him for forcing me to be eyed like a prostitute, but now I approached his

114

bed very carefully, drew up the chair, opened my handbag, and took out my cigarettes.

I smoked as I sat beside his bed, turned my eyes away from him when he began to get restless, looked at the green, heart-shaped pattern of the wallpaper, glanced up at the ugly light fixture, and blew the smoke of my cigarette through the crack of the open window. I went back over the past and realized that nothing has changed much since we got married. In those days we started our marriage in a furnished room which in terms of ugliness was in no way inferior to this hotel room. When the war broke out we had just moved into a proper apartment, but I think of it as of something that has never been: three rooms, kitchen, and bath, and clean. Clemens had a room with a Max-and-Moritz cartoon wallpaper, although he was too young to recognize pictures. By the time he was old enough to do so, the building containing a room with a Max-and-Moritz cartoon wallpaper no longer existed, and I can still see Fred standing there, his hands in the pockets of his gray uniform trousers, gazing at the pile of rubble with a plume of smoke rising from it. Fred seemed to grasp nothing, feel nothing, unable to comprehend that we no longer owned any linen, furniture, anything— he looked at me with the expression of a man who had never really owned anything. He took the burning cigarette from his lips, put it in mine, I drew on it, and with the first puff I burst into a paroxysm of laughter.

I opened the window wide and threw the cigarette butt down into the courtyard: garbage pails stood beside a big puddle, yellowed by briquet ash, my cigarette fell into it with a hiss. A train rumbled into the station. I heard the announcer's voice without understanding his words.

Fred woke up when the cathedral bells started pealing, their ringing made the windowpanes oscillate, vibrate, and this vibration was picked up by a metal curtain rod lying on the windowsill, its dance producing a subdued chittering.

Fred looked at me without moving, without saying a word, he sighed, and I knew he was slowly emerging from sleep.

"Fred," I said.

"Yes," he said, and he drew me down to him and kissed me. He drew me all the way down and we embraced, looked at each other, and when he took my head in his hands, holding it away so as to scrutinize my face, I had to smile.

"We must go to Mass," I said, "or have you been?"

"No," he said, "only for a couple of minutes. I was just in time for the Blessing."

"Then let's go."

He had been lying on the bed with his shoes on, had obviously fallen asleep without pulling up the covers, and I could see he was cold. He poured some water into the basin, rubbed his face with his wet hands, dried himself, and picked up his coat from the chair.

We went downstairs arm in arm. The three men were still standing at the counter, talking to each other without looking at us. Fred handed the room key to the landlady, who hung it on a board and asked:

"Will you be gone long?"

"An hour," said Fred.

When we reached the cathedral the service had ended, and we were just in time to see the procession of canons entering the sacristy: they looked like white carp swimming slowly through pale gray water. The Mass was being said by a tired vicar at a side altar, he said it fast, hastily, and twitched his shoulders impatiently when he moved to the left side of the altar for the Gospel and the acolyte was not there with the missal. Clouds of incense wafted across from the main altar, and many people were walking around the group that was attending Mass. Most of them were men wearing little red flags on their lapels. At the Consecration some were startled and stopped at the sound of the bell tinkling, but most of them walked on, looking at the mosaics, the windows, going up to the altars.

I had looked at the clock that hangs high up beside the organ and gives out a gentle, clear note every fifteen minutes. And as we walked to the door after the Blessing, I noticed that the Mass had lasted exactly nineteen minutes. Fred was waiting for me in the porch, I went to the altar of the Blessed Virgin, and said an Ave. I prayed not to be pregnant, although I was afraid to pray for that. Many candles were burning in front of the Virgin, and to the left of the massive iron candlestand lay a whole bundle of yellow candles. A cardboard sign had been tacked up next to them: DONATED BY THE CATHOLIC DRUGGISTS' CHAPTER OF THE GERMAN DRUGGISTS' FEDERATION.

I returned to Fred, and we went out. Outside the sun

was shining. It was twenty minutes past five, and I was hungry. I took Fred's arm, and as we walked down the wide steps I could hear him jingling the loose change in his pocket.

"Do you want to eat in a restaurant?" he asked me.

"No," I said, "at a snack bar. I like eating at snack bars."

"Then let's go," he said, and we turned into Blücher Lane. Over the years the piles of rubble have smoothed out into rounded hillocks, have subsided, and weeds grow there in dense profusion, a matted tangle of green-gray bushes with the pinkish shimmer of faded willow herb. For a while the General Blücher monument lay there in the gutter: a huge, determined bronze figure staring angrily up into the sky—until he was stolen.

Beyond a wrought-iron gateway, dirt lay piled up. Only a narrow path had been cleared through the ruins, and when we emerged onto Mommsen Street, where a few buildings are still standing, I could hear from a distance, across the rubble, the music of a fairground. I stopped Fred, and as we stood there I could hear it more distinctly: the frenzied blare of the calliope.

"Fred," I said, "is there something going on in town?"

"Yes," he said, "because of the druggists, I think. Do you want to go? Shall we go there?"

"Oh yes!" I said. We hurried on, cutting through Veleda Street, and when we turned another corner we found ourselves suddenly in the midst of the racket, the smells, of the fairground. The sounds of the barrel organs, the pungent smell of goulash mixed with the cloying, greasy smell of deep-fried pastry, the high-pitched swishing of the merry-ground, filled me with excitement. I felt my heart beating faster—those smells, that noise, all confused, yet containing a secret melody.

"Fred," I said, "give me some money."

He took the loose money from his pocket, pulled out the bank notes from among the coins, folded them, and put them in his shabby notebook. He piled all the small change onto my palm, there were some fat silver coins among them; I counted them carefully while Fred watched me with a smile.

"Six marks eighty," I said. "That's too much, Fred."

"Keep it," he said, "please," and I saw his thin, gray, careworn face, saw the snow-white cigarette between his pale lips, and knew that I loved him. I have often wondered why I love him; I don't really know, there are many reasons, but one I do know: because it's fun to go to the fair with him.

"But then I'll pay for the meal," I said.

"Whatever you say," he replied. I took his arm, drew him across to the goulash booth, its front painted with dancing Hungarians—peasant boys in round hats, hands on hips, leaping around the girls. We propped our elbows on the counter, and the woman sitting on a folding chair beside the steaming pot got up and approached us with a smile.

She was stout, with dark hair, and her strong, handsome hands were covered with cheap rings. Around her tawny neck she wore a black velvet ribbon with a medallion dangling from it.

"Two goulash," I said, pushing two marks across to her.

We exchanged smiles, Fred and I, while the woman went to the back and lifted the lid from the pot.

"I've already had some goulash today," Fred said.

"Oh, I'm sorry," I replied.

"Never mind, I like goulash." He put his hand on my arm.

The woman dipped her ladle deep down into the pot, brought it up piled high with goulash, and the steam rising from the pot misted the mirrors on the rear wall. She handed each of us a roll, then wiped the mirror with a cloth, and said to me: "So you can see how beautiful you are." I looked into the flat mirror and saw that I really did look beautiful: far behind my face I saw the blurred reflection of a shooting gallery, beyond the shooting gallery the carrousel swing. I was shocked when in the back of the mirror my glance fell on Fred: he can't eat anything hot, it hurts his gums; the way he turns the food over in his mouth until it has cooled off, the expression of mild annoyance, of impatience—all this gives his face a sort of old-fogey, senile look that shocks me more each time. But the mirror misted over again, the woman slowly stirred her ladle around in the pot, and it seemed to me that she gave less to those standing beside us than she had given to us.

We pushed away our empty plates, thanked her, and left. I took Fred's arm again, and we strolled slowly through the lanes between the booths. I threw empty cans at dolls with fixed grins, rejoiced when I hit their heads, when they flipped over backward against brown sacking, when the hidden mechanism jerked them upright again. I happily let myself be deceived by the droning voice of a barker, bought a lottery ticket, watched the wheel of fortune turning, kept glancing at the big yellow teddy bear I was hoping to win, have been hoping to win since I was a child. The wheel's rattling pointer notched its way slowly through the cordon of nails, halted just before my number, and I didn't win the bear, didn't win anything.

I flung myself onto the narrow seat of the carrousel swing, pressed twenty pfennigs into a dirty palm, let myself be swung up and around on the chains, slowly, higher and higher, around the calliope that was concealed in the wooden bowels of the center support and blared its frenzied tune into my face. I saw the cathedral spire beyond the ruins fly right through me, way off in the distance the dull, dense green of the weeds, saw the tent roofs with their rain puddles; and over and over again, in the vortex of the whirling carrousel that was whipping me around for twenty pfennigs, I flung myself into the midst of the sun, its glare struck me like a blow every time I touched it. I heard the hum of the chain, the shrieks of women, saw the steam, the whirling dust of the fairground, raced through that greasy, cloying smell, and when I staggered down the wooden steps again I sank into Fred's arms and said: "Oh, Fred!"

For ten pfennigs we could have one dance, on a

wooden platform. Surrounded by teen-agers vigorously swaying their hips, we held each other close, and whenever I revolved with Fred in the rhythm of the dance I found myself looking into the fat, lecherous face of a trumpet player whose soiled collar was only half hidden by his instrument—and each time he lifted his head, winked at me, and blew a shrill note out of his trumpet that seemed to be aimed at me.

I watched Fred play roulette for ten pfennigs, felt the silent tension of the men standing around when the croupier gave the wheel a spin and the ball began to bounce. The speed with which they placed their stakes, with which Fred, too, threw his coin onto exactly the right spot, seemed to indicate a skill, a mutual understanding, that I had never suspected. I saw how, as the ball rolled, the croupier raised his head and his cold eyes roamed contemptuously over the fairground. He did not lower his hard, handsome little face until the whirring began to subside, then he picked up the stakes, slid them into his pocket, tossed the coins to the winners, fumbled among the coins in his pocket, called for the players to place their stakes, observed the fingers of the men standing around, gave the wheel a contemptuous twist, lifted his head, pursed his lips, and looked around in boredom.

Twice the coins piled up in front of Fred, and he picked up the money from the table and pushed his way through to me.

We sat down on the dirty steps of a show tent with blue curtains, watched the milling crowds, swallowed the dust, and listened to the discordant concert of the calliopes, we heard the hoarse cries of the brakemen who were collecting the money. I looked at the ground, which was covered with dirt, littered with paper, cigarette butts, trampled flowers, torn tickets, and as I slowly raised my eyes I saw our children. Bellermann was holding Clemens by the hand, the girl was holding Carla's, the baby was in the carrier between Bellermann and the girl. The children had big yellow suckers in their mouths, I saw them laugh, look around, saw them stop at the shooting gallery. Bellermann went closer, Clemens took the handle of the carrier while Bellermann picked up a gun. Clemens looked over Bellermann's shoulder through the sight. The children seemed happy, they were laughing now as Bellermann stuck a red paper flower in the girl's hair. They turned off to the right, I saw Bellermann count out some money into Clemens' palm, saw my son's lips moving, counting to himself, saw him raise his hand with a little smile and thank Bellermann.

"Let's go," I whispered to Fred, stood up and pulled up his coat collar, "our children are here."

"Where are they?" he said. We looked at each other, between us, in those twelve inches of air between our eyes, were the thousand nights when we had made love. Fred took his cigarette from his mouth and asked hesitantly: "So what are we going to do?"

"I don't know," I said. He drew me off into a lane between the show tent and an idle merry-go-round whose curved sides were draped with green canvas. We looked silently at the tent pegs that held the ropes.

"Come in here," said Fred, holding open a gap be-

123

tween two green canvas flaps. He squeezed his way in, then helped me inside, and we sat down in the dark, Fred on a great wooden swan, I beside him on a rocking horse. Fred's pale face was cut in half by a streak of light coming through the gap in the canvas.

"Maybe," said Fred, "I should never have married."

"Nonsense," I said. "Don't give me that. That's what all men say." I looked at him and added: "And how flattering for me too—but then what woman succeeds in making a marriage bearable?"

"You've been more successful than most women," he said, and he lifted his face from the swan's head and put his hand on my arm. "Fifteen years now that we've been married, and. . . ."

"A splendid marriage," I said.

"Magnificent," he said, "really magnificent." He took his hand off my arm, laid both hands on the swan's head and his face on top, and looked wearily up at me. "I'm sure you and the kids are happier without me."

"That's not true," I said. "If you only knew. . . ."

"If I only knew what?"

"Fred," I said. "Every day the children ask for you ten times, and I lie there every night, almost every night, and cry."

"You cry?" he said, lifted his face again and looked at me, and I was sorry I had said that.

"I'm saying it not to tell you that I cry but just so you know how wrong you are."

Sunlight fell suddenly through the gap, was sucked into the whole circular space as if through a green filter, and its golden light revealed the figures of the merry-go-round: grinning horses, green dragons, swans, ponies, and behind us I saw a wedding coach upholstered in red velvet and drawn by two white horses.

"Come on," I said to Fred, "we'll be more comfortable in there."

He climbed down from his swan, helped me off my rocking horse, and we sat side by side on the soft velvet of the coach. The sun had disappeared again, we were surrounded by the gray shadows of the animals.

"You're crying," said Fred. He looked at me, was about to put his arm around me but drew it back again. "Are you crying because I've left you?"

"Because of that," I said softly, "but not only because of that. You know I'm happier when you're with us. But I can see too that you can't stand it—and sometimes it's just as well you're not there. I was afraid of you, afraid of your face when you struck the children, I was afraid of your voice, and I wouldn't want you to come back like that and for everything to go on the way it was before you left. I'd rather lie in bed and cry than know you are beating the children simply and solely because we have no money. That's why you beat the children, isn't it, because we're poor?"

"Yes," he said, "being poor has made me ill."

"Yes," I said, "that's why it's better if you stay away —unless things change completely. Just let me cry. In another year I'll have reached the point—maybe reached the point—where I too beat the children, where I'll be like one of those poor women the very sight of whom used to scare me as a child: hoarse and poor, dragged along by the ruthless terror of life, in the canyons of filthy tenements, either beating their children or stuffing them with candy, at night spreading themselves open to the embrace of some wretched drunk who comes home smelling of fried-sausage booths, bringing along in his pocket two crumpled cigarettes which they smoke, smoke side by side in the dark when the lovemaking is over. Oh, how I despised them, those women—may God not punish me for that—give me another cigarette, Fred."

He quickly drew the pack from his pocket, held it out to me, took one for himself, and when the match flared up I saw his poor face in the greenish twilight of the merry-go-round.

"Go on," he said, "please go on."

"Perhaps I'm also crying because I'm pregnant."

"You're pregnant?"

"Perhaps," I said. "You know what I'm like when I'm pregnant. I still don't believe I am. Otherwise I'd have felt sick on the carrousel. I pray every day that I may not be pregnant. Or would you like another child?"

"No, no," he said hastily.

"But if it comes, you're the father; oh Fred," I said, "it's not nice to hear that." I was sorry I had said that.

He said nothing, looked at me, sat leaning back in the coach and smoking, and only said: "Go on, please go on. Tell me everything."

"I'm also crying," I said, "because the children are so quiet. They're so silent, Fred. The way they take it for granted that they have to go to school, and take it all so seriously—it scares me, and the conscientious way they do their homework—that scares me too. The stupid way kids carry on about their tests, almost the same words I used myself when I was their age. It's so frightening, Fred. The pleasure in their faces when they smell the skimpy pot roast simmering on the stove, the quiet way they pack their satchels every morning, hoist them on their backs, their sandwiches in their lunch bags. As they go off to school, I often creep out into the corridor, Fred, stand at the window, and follow them with my eyes as long as I can see them: their slender backs, hollowed a bit from the weight of the books, there they go, walking side by side as far as the corner where Clemens turns off, and I can watch Carla a bit longer as she strolls along gray Mozart Street, with your walk, Fred, her hands in her coat pockets, deep in thought perhaps about a knitting pattern or the date of Charlemagne's death. It makes me cry because their eagerness reminds me of the eagerness of children I hated when I was in school—those children are so like the Child Jesus in pictures of the Holy Family, playing beside Joseph's carpentry bench, mild, gentle curly-haired creatures, eleven or ten years old, casually dropping long curling wood shavings through their fingers. Wood shavings that exactly match their own curly locks."

"Our children," he said softly, "look like the Child Jesus in pictures of the Holy Family?"

I looked at him. "No," I said. "No—but when I see

127

them strolling along like that they have something of
that hopelessly senseless humility that makes me weep
tears of fear and defiance."

"Good God," he said. "But that's nonsense—I think
you simply envy them because they're children."

"No, no, Fred," I said. "I'm scared because I can't
protect them from anything, not from the callousness
of humanity, the callousness of Mrs. Franke, who for
all her receiving the Body of Christ every morning
comes dashing out of her office whenever one of the
children has used the toilet to check the state of the
toilet and starts yapping in the corridor if a single drop
of water has landed on her wallpaper. I'm scared of the
drops of water—whenever I hear the children flushing
the toilet I break out in a sweat—I can't really say,
maybe you know, what made me so sad."

"What makes you sad is that we're poor. It's very
simple. And there's nothing I can do to comfort you:
there is no escape. I can't promise you that some day
we'll have more money or anything. Oh, you'd be surprised how nice it is to live in a clean house, to have
absolutely no money worries . . . you'd be surprised."

"In fact I can remember," I said, "that in my parents'
home everything was always clean, the rent was always
paid on time, and as for money—well, even we, Fred,
you remember. . . ."

"I remember," he broke in, "but I haven't much feeling for the past. My memory consists of holes, big holes
held together by a delicate, very delicate web like very
thin wire. Of course I remember—we once had an

apartment, even our own bathroom, money to pay for everything—what was I doing in those days?"

"Fred," I said, "you don't remember what you were doing in those days?"

"It's true," he said, "I can't remember...." He put his arm around me.

"You were working in a wallpaper factory."

"Of course," he said. "My clothes smelled of paste, and I used to bring home faulty sample books for Clemens, and he would tear them up in his crib. I remember, but it couldn't have lasted long."

"Two years," I said, "till the war came."

"Of course," he said, "then came the war. Maybe you'd have been better off marrying a capable man, one of those really hardworking fellows with some respect for culture."

"Stop it," I said.

"You would have sat together in the evening, poring over fine books, the way you love to do—the kids' bedroom would have been furnished in the latest style —a Nefertiti on the wall and the Isenheim Altar on wooden panels, and Van Gogh's *Sunflowers*—a first-rate print, of course—above the parents' bed next to a Madonna of Beuron, and a recorder in a red case, sturdy but exquisite of course—right? Oh how that crap has always bored me, tasteful homes bore me, and I don't know why. What is it you really want?" he suddenly asked.

I looked at him, and for the first time since I have known him I felt that he was angry. "I don't know what I want," I said, and flung my cigarette down on the wooden floor beside the coach, stamping it out. "I don't know what I want, but I've said nothing about Nefertiti, nothing about the Isenheim Altar, although I have nothing against them, I've said nothing about capable men because I hate capable men, I can't think of anything more boring than capable men, they're so capable their breath stinks of it. But I'd really like to know what there is that you do take seriously. Nothing, nothing that other men take seriously, and then there are a few things that you take more seriously than anyone else. You have no profession—pharmaceutical agent, photographer, then you worked in a library—it was pitiful to see you in a library because you didn't even know how to hold a book properly—then a wallpaper factory, a shipper, right? As for being a switchboard operator—you learned that during the war."

"Oh, stop talking about the war!" he said. "It bores me."

"O.K.," I said. "Your entire life, our entire life, ever since I've been with you, has been spent at snack stands, at goulash booths, in filthy taverns, fifth-rate hotels, on fairgrounds, and in that rotten hole we've been living in for eight years."

"And in churches," he said.

"In churches, O.K.," I said.

"Don't forget the cemeteries."

"I'm not forgetting the cemeteries, but never, even when we were on trips, have you shown the slightest interest in culture."

"Culture," he said. "If you can tell me what that is—

no, I'm not interested in it. I'm interested in God, in cemeteries, in you, snack bars, fairgrounds, and fifth-rate hotels."

"Don't forget alcohol," I said.

"No, I'm not forgetting alcohol, I'll throw in movies for good measure, if you like, and pinball machines."

"And our children," I said.

"Yes, the children. I love them very much, more perhaps than you suspect—I really do love them very much. But I'm nearly forty-four, and I can't tell you how tired I am—think about that," he said, and he suddenly looked at me and asked: "Are you cold, shall we leave?"

"No, no," I said, "go on, please go on."

"Oh, what's the use," he said, "let's stop. Why bother —let's not quarrel, you know me, must know me, and you know I'm a bad bargain, and at my age it's too late to change. No one ever changes. The only thing in my favor is that I love you."

"Yes," I said. "You're not much to write home about."

"Shall we go now?" he asked.

"No," I said, "let's stay here for a bit. Or are you cold?"

"No," he said, "but I'd like to go back to the hotel with you."

"In a minute," I said, "but first there are a few more things you must tell me about. Or don't you want to?"

"Go ahead, ask," he replied.

I leaned my head on his chest, saying nothing, and we both listened to the sounds from the calliope, the shrieks of the carrousel riders, and the hoarse barks of the brakemen.

"Fred," I asked, "are you eating properly? Open your mouth a minute." I turned my head, he opened his mouth, I saw the red, inflamed gums, touched his teeth and felt how loose they were. "Periodontosis," I said. "In a year you'll have to have dentures."

"Do you really think so?" he asked anxiously. He stroked my hair and added: "We've forgotten about the kids." We fell silent again, listening to the noise coming from outside, and I said: "They'll be all right, I'm not worried about the kids, for a minute I was—they'll be all right going around with that young couple. Nothing's going to happen to them. Fred," I murmured, snuggling my head onto his chest, "where exactly are you living?"

"With the Blocks," he replied. "On Escher Street."

"Blocks," I said, "I don't know them."

"You don't know the Blocks?" he asked. "The people who used to live downstairs in Father's building, the ones who had the stationery store?"

"Oh those," I said. "He had such funny blond curls and didn't smoke. That's where you're staying?"

"For the past month. I ran across him in a bar, and he took me home when I was drunk. I've been staying with them ever since."

"Do they have room for you?"

He didn't answer. The show tent next to us was now opening for business, someone started banging a triangle, and a hoarse voice shouted through a megaphone:

"Step up! Step up! Something for the boys!"

"Fred," I asked, "didn't you hear me?"

"I heard you. The Blocks have plenty of room. They've got thirteen rooms."

"Thirteen rooms?"

"Yes," he said. "Old Block is a watchman there, the house has been empty for three months, it belongs to some Englishman, called Stripper I think, he's a general or a gangster, or both, or maybe something else for all I know, he's been away for three months, and the Blocks are looking after the house. They have to take care of the lawn so that it looks tiptop even in winter: every day old Block goes through that huge garden with a bunch of rollers and lawnmowers, and every three days a bale of artificial manure arrives: it's a fantastic setup, I tell you—a lot of bathrooms and things —four I believe, and sometimes I'm even allowed to have a bath. There's a library which even has books, lots of books, and even if I know nothing about culture I do know about books, they're good books, marvelous books, many many books—and a drawing room or whatever it's called—then there's a den, a dining room, a room for the dog, two bedrooms upstairs, one for the gangster or whatever he is, one for his wife, three for guests. Of course they also have a kitchen, one, two, and. . . ."

"Stop it, Fred," I said, "please stop."

"Oh no," he said, "I won't stop. I never told you about it, my love, because I didn't want to torment you, I really didn't, but now it's better for you to hear me out. I have to talk about the house, I dream about it, I get drunk to forget about it, but even when I'm drunk I can't forget it: how many rooms did I tell you about, eight or nine? I don't remember. There are thirteen—you should just see the room for the dog. It's slightly larger than ours, but only a bit, I don't want to be unfair, maybe it's ten square feet larger, definitely not more, we want to be fair, there's nothing like being fair. We'll inscribe the word 'fairness' on our modest banner, won't we, dear heart?"

"Oh, Fred," I said, "you do mean to torment me."

"Me torment you? Oh you don't understand! I wouldn't dream of tormenting you, but I have to talk about the house—I really do. The doghouse is a pagoda, as large as the buffets in these homes of the cultural elite. As well as the four bathrooms there are also a few shower stalls, I haven't counted those: I want to be fair, I want to get drunk on fairness. I will never count a shower stall as a room, that would be unjust, and we do want to inscribe justice beside fairness on our modest banner. All that's not the worst, dear heart—but the heart is vacant—oh how wonderful those spreading lawns are behind those great villas, if only a child were allowed to play on them—or even a dog. We must plant spreading lawns for our dogs, my love. But this house is empty, this lawn is never used, if I may be permitted to apply that dirty word here. Bedrooms: empty. Guest rooms: empty—downstairs everything empty. In the attic there are three more rooms, one for the housekeeper, one for the cook, one for the manservant, and the good lady has already complained because of course the maid needs a room and now has to sleep in a guest room. We must remember that, my love, when we build our house and hoist our banner of justice and fairness on it. . . ."

"Fred," I said, "I can't take any more."

"Yes you can, you've borne five children, and you can. I must finish. I can't stop now, you can leave if you want, although I would've liked to be with you, tonight, but if you don't want to listen you can leave. I've been living for a month in this house, and I simply have to talk to you about it, you, the very person I would have gladly spared. I wanted to spare you, dear heart, but you asked me and now you must hear the whole answer. The good lady actually did make a kind of suicide attempt because she lacks this room for the maid. You can imagine what a sensitive person she is, and the kind of worries she has to endure. But now they've gone away, they've been gone three months, they usually spend about nine months of the year away—the old gangster or whatever who lives there happens to be a Dante scholar, one of the few genuine Dante scholars still around. One of the few to be taken seriously, just like our Bishop—a fact which I hope you, as an educated Christian, are aware of. For nine months of the year the house is empty, during that time old Block stands guard over the lawn and looks after it— obviously, since there's nothing more splendid than a manicured lawn. The floor of the dog's room mustn't be waxed. And no children are allowed in the house."

"Step up, folks, step up!" the hoarse voice next door was shouting, "something for the boys: Manuela, the sweetest young thing this side of heaven!"

"Fred," I whispered, "why aren't children allowed in the house?"

"No children are allowed in the house because the wife doesn't like them. She detests children, and she senses it when any have been there, smells it even after nine months. Block's predecessor was a disabled veteran who once let his two grandchildren play there: in the basement, of course, quite properly, certainly not on the lawn. The man let them play in the basement, and when the wife came back she found out, and he was fired. That's why Block has been so careful. For I asked him once whether my kids couldn't visit me one day: he turned white as a sheet. I'm allowed to live there because I'm supposed to be helping look after the lawn, because I keep the heating system in good shape. I have a little cubbyhole downstairs off the hall, it's really a cloakroom; when I wake up in the morning my eyes fall on an old Dutch painting—soft old colors: some inn or other. I've felt like pinching one of them— there are some more in the library—but they'd notice right away, of course, and it wouldn't be fair to Block either."

"Manuela will sing about love!" shouted the voice next door.

"Block even thinks the wife is a lesbian."

"Oh Fred, won't you stop, shouldn't we go to the hotel?"

"Just one more minute," he said, "you have to listen

136

to me for one more minute, then I'll be through and you'll know where I live, and how I live. Sometimes the Bishop drops by in the evenings. He's the only person allowed in the house, the entire Dante literature is at his disposal. Block has orders to make him comfortable, keep him warm, draw the curtains, and I've seen him more than once, the Bishop: serene enjoyment in his face, a book in his hand, the teapot beside him, notebook and pencil. His chauffeur sits downstairs with us in the basement, smoking a pipe, goes outside now and again to keep an eye on the car. When he's ready to leave the Bishop rings the bell, the chauffeur jumps to his feet, and Block goes outside too, lets himself be called 'my good man,' gets his tip. That's all," said Fred. "Now we can go, if you like. Do you want to go?"

I shook my head, unable to speak: my tears were choking me. I was so tired, and still the sun was shining outside, and everything Fred had told me seemed to me so false because I sensed the hatred in his voice. And next door the voice shouted through the megaphone: "You're just in time, gentlemen, to see Manuela, to hear her, the little darling who is going to break your hearts!"

We could hear somebody climbing onto the merry-go-round on the other side. Fred looked at me: a door in the center column was opened and slammed shut, a light was turned on, and suddenly the calliope in the bowels of the merry-go-round started up. Light streamed in as invisible hands began to roll up the canvas, and in the center column a window opened, a pale man with a very long face looked at us and said: "Care for a ride, folks? The first ride's free, of course." He removed his cap, blond hair fell over his forehead, he scratched his head, replaced his cap, and looked at me calmly, his face was sad, although he was smiling, then he looked at Fred and said: "No, I don't think your wife would like it."

"Really?" said Fred.

"No, she wouldn't like it," he tried to smile at me but without success, and shrugged his shoulders. Fred looked at me. The man shut the window, came around the calliope toward us, and stopped beside us: he was tall, the sleeves of his jacket were too short, and his thin, muscular arms looked very white. He gave me a searching look and said: "I'm sure—no, your wife wouldn't like it. But I can wait, if you want to rest a bit longer."

"Oh, no," I said, "we've got to go."

Meanwhile the canvas flaps had been rolled up, a few children were climbing onto the horses, onto the swans. We got up and stepped down. The man took off his cap, gave us a last wave, and called out: "Good luck, then, good luck!"

"Thanks," I called back. Fred didn't say a word. We walked slowly across the fairground, without looking back. Fred held my arm closer and led me to Mommsen Street. We walked slowly through the rubble sites, past the cathedral, and toward the hotel. It was still quiet in the streets around the station, and the sun was still shining, its bright light showing up the dust that lay on the weeds in the ruins.

Without warning, the rhythm of the carrousel rose up in me, and I began to feel faint.

"Fred," I whispered, "I have to lie down, or sit down."

I saw his alarm. He put his arm around me, and led me into a ruined building: fire-blackened walls surrounded us, high walls: X-RAY LABORATORY TO THE LEFT, it said somewhere. Fred led me through a door opening, sat me down on the remains of a wall, and I watched apathetically as he took off his coat. Then he made me lie down, cushioning my head on his folded coat. Under my body it felt smooth and cool: I groped along the edge of the masonry, felt the tiles, and whispered: "I shouldn't have gone on the carrousel, but I do love it so. I just love going on the carrousel."

"Can I get you something?" Fred asked softly. "Some coffee maybe, it's not far to the station."

"No," I said, "just stay with me. I'm sure I'll be able to walk to the hotel in a few minutes. Just stay with me, Fred."

"Yes," he said, putting his hand on my forehead.

I looked at the gray-green wall, smudged with red clay where a statue had been smashed, and an inscription which I could no longer decipher, for now I was turning, slowly, at first, in a circle, with my feet forming the fixed center of the circle that my body was now describing faster and faster. It was a bit like at the circus where the pretty girl is held by her feet and whirled around by a powerful gladiator.

At first I could still make out the greenish wall with the red clay smudge of the statue, and on the other side the white light in the window opening; it flickered green and white before my eyes, but the borderlines soon blurred, the colors ran into each other, the palest blend of green and white rotated in front of me, I in front of it, I didn't know which, until the colors ran together in that frantic speed and I was revolving parallel to the ground in an almost colorless shimmering. Not until the motion slowed down did I notice that I was not moving, only my head, my head seemed to be revolving, at times it seemed to be lying beside my body, without any connection to it, then at my feet, and only for brief moments where it belonged, attached to the top of my neck.

My head seemed to be rolling around my body, but that couldn't be true either, I groped for my chin with my hands, felt it, the bony lump: even during the moments when my head seemed to be lying at my feet I could feel my chin. Maybe it was only my eyes that were revolving, I didn't know, the only thing real was the nausea, an acrid acidity that rose in my throat as if it were a barometer, then dropping back only to rise again slowly. It was no use closing my eyes either: when I did, not only was my head turning, I could feel my chest and legs joining those crazy circles, they all formed their circles, an insane ballet that made the nausea even more acute.

But when I kept my eyes open I could tell that the section of wall always stayed the same: a fragment of green-painted wall with a chocolate-colored border at the top and some words I couldn't make out painted dark brown on the light green. Sometimes the letters shrank like the microscopic letters on oculists' charts, then they would swell, repulsive dark-brown sausages spreading outward so fast that their meaning, their shape, could no longer be grasped, they would burst, become a brown blur on the wall, denying all legibility, then a moment later shrink again till they became tiny as flyspecks—but they didn't disappear.

The engine that was turning me around was the nausea—that was the pivot of this carrousel, and it was a shock to suddenly realize that I was lying quite flat, on the same spot as before, without having moved an inch. I realized this when the nausea subsided for a moment: everything was quiet, everything was in its proper place again—I saw my chest, the dirty brown leather of my shoes, and my eyes fell on the writing on the wall which I could now read: YOUR PHYSICIAN WILL HELP YOU IF GOD HELPS HIM.

I closed my eyes, the word GOD remained with me, first it seemed to be in writing, three large, dark-brown letters behind my closed lids, then I no longer saw the writing, and it stayed with me as a WORD, sank into me, seemed to fall deeper and deeper without touching bottom, and suddenly it was up at the surface with me, not writing, just word: GOD.

GOD seemed to be the only one staying with me in this nausea that was flooding my heart, filling my veins, circulating in me like my blood—cold sweat broke out on me and a mortal fear—there had been moments when I had thought of Fred, of the children, had seen my mother's face, the babies, just as I see them in the mirror—but they all floated away on this tide of nausea—indifference toward them all filled me and I was left with nothing but the word GOD.

I wept, saw no more, thought of nothing else but that single word; hot, swift tears flowed from my eyes onto my face, and from the way the tears fell without my feeling them on my chin or neck I could tell that I was now lying on my side—and once again I raced around, faster than ever—then suddenly lay quite still, and I leaned over the edge of the broken wall and vomited into the dusty green weeds. . . .

Fred held my forehead as he has so often done.

"Feeling better now?" he asked gently.

"Yes, I'm feeling better," I said. He carefully wiped my mouth with his handkerchief. "Only I'm so tired."

"You can sleep now," said Fred, "it's only a few steps to the hotel."

"Yes, sleep," I said.

II

The sallowness of her face was tinged with a darker tone, making her skin appear almost brown; the whites of her eyes, too, were badly discolored. I poured her some lemonade, she drank it all, took my hand, and held it against her forehead.

"Shall I get a doctor?" I asked.

"No," she said, "I'm all right now. It was the baby. It was resisting our legacy of curses, the poverty that's waiting for it."

"Resisting," I went on, "becoming the future customer of a druggist, becoming a cherished parishioner. But I will cherish it."

"Perhaps," she said, "he will be a bishop, not a parishioner at all, perhaps a Dante scholar."

"Oh, Käte, don't try to be funny."

"I'm not trying to be funny. How do you know how our children will turn out? Maybe they'll have hearts of stone, build pagodas for their dogs, and detest children. Perhaps the woman who detests children was one of fifteen who used to live in less space than her

143

dog now has. Maybe she is . . ." Käte broke off, a loud rat-a-tat had started up outside: bursts and bangs like explosions. I ran to the window and pushed it open. The noises contained the whole war: the rumble of aircraft, the bark of explosions; the sky turned dark gray, covered now with snow-white parachutes that slowly carried down big, flapping red flags that bore the words: GRISS RUBBER—PROTECTS AND PREVENTS! Past the cathedral spires, onto the station roof, down into the streets they floated, the flags, and here and there I could hear the jubilant cries of children into whose hands a flag, a parachute, had fallen.

"What's going on?" asked Käte from the bed.

"Oh, nothing," I said, "some advertising gimmick."

But now came a whole squadron of planes: they roared overhead, with sinister elegance: low over the roofs, gray wings tilting, and the noise of their engines aimed at our hearts and found their mark. I saw Käte beginning to tremble, ran to her bed, and held her hand.

"Oh God, what's that?"

We heard the planes circle over the city, then elegantly fly away again, their droning faded toward an invisible horizon, and the whole sky over the city was covered with great red birds sinking slowly, slowly to the ground: they covered the sky like a tattered sunset, great red rubber birds which we couldn't identify until they reached the level of the buildings: they were storks with broken necks, down they fluttered with dangling legs, their limp heads hung down gruesomely as if a company of the hanged were descending from the sky: down they sailed through the gray evening sky, repulsive little red rubber clouds, mute and hideous. From the streets rose the sound of children rejoicing. Käte pressed my hand. I leaned over and kissed her.

"Fred," she said in a low voice, "I've made debts."

"Who cares?" I said, "I make debts too."

"Many?"

"Yes, many. Now there isn't a soul left who will lend me anything. There's nothing harder than trying to raise fifty marks in a city of three hundred thousand people. Just thinking about it makes me sweat."

"But you're tutoring, aren't you?"

"Yes," I said, "but I smoke a lot."

"Are you drinking again?"

"Yes, but not that often, my love. Since I left you I've only been really drunk twice. Is that a lot?"

"It's not a lot," she said. "I can understand your drinking. But perhaps you could try not to do it any more. It's so pointless. During the war you hardly drank at all."

"During the war it was different," I said. "During the war I got drunk on boredom. You wouldn't believe how drunk you can get on boredom, afterward you lie in bed, everything spins before your eyes. Try drinking three pails of lukewarm water, you'll find yourself drunk on water—it's the same with boredom. You wouldn't believe how boring the war was. Sometimes I'd think about you and the kids, I phoned you as often as I could just to hear your voice. It was bitter to hear you, but that bitterness was better than being drunk on boredom."

"You've never told me much about the war."

"It's not worth the effort, my love. Just imagine, all day long at the phone, almost always only the voices of senior officers. You can't imagine how ridiculous senior officers are on the phone. Their vocabulary is so limited, a hundred and twenty to a hundred and forty words, I'd say. That's not enough for six years of war. Day after day, eight hours at the phone: report—action—action—report—deploy—to the last man—command—field report—report to H.Q.—action—to the very last man—resist—Führer—don't weaken. Then a bit of gossip—women. And then try to imagine the barracks: I was a switchboard operator in barracks for almost three years—I'd like to spend years puking boredom. And if I'd wanted to go out and get drunk, wherever I went: uniforms. I could never stand the sight of uniforms, you know that."

"I know," she said.

"There was one lieutenant I knew who recited Rilke to his girl over the phone. I could've died, although it was a bit of a change. Some of them sang too, taught each other songs over the phone, but most of them sent death over the phone—it wiggled through the wires, with their thin voices they barked it into the receiver, into the ear of some other fellow who had to make sure enough people died. If only a few died, the senior officers usually felt the action had been badly executed. It's not for nothing that the greatness of a battle is measured by the number of dead. The dead were not boring, my love, nor were the cemeteries."

I lay down beside her on the bed, pulled up the cover.

Downstairs the musicians were tuning their instruments, and from the bar came the sound of a man singing, somber and beautiful, and then a woman's hoarse, wild cry would break into the man's singing: we couldn't make out the words, but it was an antiphony of rhythmic beauty. Trains were rumbling into the station, and the voice of the announcer came to us through the deepening dusk like the gentle murmurings of a friend.

"You don't feel like dancing now, do you?"

"Oh no," she said, "it's so nice just to lie quiet for once. I'd like it if you could just give Mrs. Röder a call to see whether everything is all right. And I'd like something to eat, Fred. But first tell me something else. Maybe you'd explain why you married me."

"Because of breakfast," I said. "I was looking for someone I could have breakfast with all my life, so my choice—that's what it's called, isn't it?—fell on you. You've been a marvelous breakfast partner. And I've never been bored with you. Nor you with me, I hope."

"No," she said. "I've never been bored with you."

"But now you cry at night when you're alone. Wouldn't it be better if I came back, even the way things are?"

She looked at me without answering. I kissed her hands, her neck, but she turned away and looked silently at the wallpaper. The singing in the bar had stopped, but now the dance band was playing, and we could hear the sounds of people dancing downstairs in the lounge. I lit a cigarette. Käte was still looking at the wall, saying nothing.

"You must understand," I said gently, "I obviously

can't leave you alone if you really are pregnant. But I don't know whether I'll find the strength to be as forbearing as I should. But I do love you, I hope you don't doubt that."

"I don't doubt it," she said, without turning around, "I really don't."

I wanted to embrace her, grasp her by the shoulders, turn her toward me, but I suddenly knew I mustn't.

"If something like just now should happen again," I said, "you can't be alone, can you?"

"I'd hate to count the curses aimed at me when the others in the apartment find out I'm pregnant. You've no idea how terrible it is to be pregnant. When I was expecting the baby, Fred, you remember. . . ."

"I remember," I said, "it was terrible, it was summertime, and I didn't have a cent, not even enough to buy you a bottle of soda pop."

"And I was so lethargic," she said, "I enjoyed being a real slattern. I had a terrific urge to spit on the floor in front of people."

"You actually did."

"Right," she said, "I spat on the ground at Mrs. Franke's feet when she asked me how far along I was. It's especially charming when someone asks you how far along you are."

"That's why we didn't get the apartment."

"No, we didn't get the apartment because you drink."

"Do you really think so?"

"Absolutely, Fred. A pregnant woman is forgiven

a lot of things. Oh, I was bad-tempered and dirty, and I enjoyed being bad-tempered and dirty."

"It would be nice if you could turn around again, I see you so rarely."

"Oh don't," she said. "It's lovely, lying here like this. And I'm still thinking about what answer I should give you."

"Take your time," I said. "I'll get something to eat and make that call. Do you want anything to drink?"

"Yes, some beer please, Fred. And give me your cigarette."

She reached her hand over her shoulder, I gave her my cigarette, and got up. She was still lying with her face to the wall and smoking as I left the room.

The corridor was filled with noise, and I could hear them squealing downstairs in the lounge as they were dancing. I caught myself trying to walk down the stairs in time with the music. The only light came from the little naked bulb. It was dark outside. In the bar there were only a few people sitting at the tables; behind the bar sat a different woman. She was older than the landlady, took off her glasses as I approached, and laid down her newspaper in a puddle of beer. The paper became saturated, turned dark. The woman blinked at me.

"Can we have something to eat?" I asked. "For room number eleven?"

"You mean, sent up?"

I nodded.

"Can't be done," she said. "We don't provide room

service. It's a sloppy habit, eating in one's room."

"Oh," I said, "I didn't know that. But my wife is ill."

"Ill?" she said. "That's all we need. Nothing serious, I hope, nothing infectious?"

"No," I said, "she's just feeling sick, my wife."

She picked up the paper from the beer puddle, shook it out, and calmly laid it on the radiator. Then she turned toward me with a shrug.

"All right, what do you want—there's nothing hot for another hour." She took a plate from the dumbwaiter behind her, and went to the glass case containing the cold food. I followed her, chose two chops, two meatballs, and asked for some bread.

"Bread?" she said. "Why bread? Why not some salad, some potato salad?

"We'd rather have bread," I said. "It's probably better for my wife."

"Women who feel sick shouldn't be taken to a hotel," she said, but she went to the dumbwaiter and called into the shaft: "Bread—a few slices of bread." A voice came back through the shaft, muffled and ominous: "Bread." The woman turned around: "It'll take a minute."

"I'd like to use the phone," I said.

"To call a doctor?"

"No," I said. She pushed the telephone across the counter. Before dialing I said: "Two beers, please, and a schnapps right now." I dialed Mrs. Röder's number, heard it ring, and waited. The woman pushed the schnapps across the counter, carried an empty beer glass to the tap.

150

"Hello," came Mrs. Röder's voice over the phone. "Hello—who it it?"

"Bogner," I said.

"Oh, it's you."

"Would you mind," I said, "just. . . ."

"Everything's all right. I've just been upstairs. The children are very happy, they've been to the fair with that young couple. They've even got some balloons. They've only just got back. Red storks, wonderful, genuine rubber, life-size."

"Are the Frankes back yet?"

"No, they'll be back later, maybe tomorrow morning."

"So everything's really all right?"

"Really," she said. "You don't have to worry. Say hello to your wife. How do you like the new lipstick?"

"Great," I said. "Thanks a lot then."

"Don't mention it," she said. "Good-bye."

I said "Good-bye," hung up, finished the schnapps, and watched the second glass of beer slowly filling. The dumbwaiter rumbled into sight, revealed a plate with four slices of white bread.

I took the two glasses up first and placed them on the chair beside Käte's bed. She was still lying there, staring at the wallpaper. I said: "Everything's all right at home—the kids are playing with those storks."

But Käte merely nodded and didn't answer.

When I brought the plate of food, she was still lying there looking at the wall, but one of the glasses was half empty.

"I'm so thirsty," she said.

"Go ahead, drink." I sat down beside her on the bed. She took two clean towels from her bag, spread them out on the chair, and we ate the meat and the bread off the clean towels and drank our beer.

"I must have some more to eat, Fred," she looked at me and smiled. "Now I don't know whether I'm eating so much because I know I'm pregnant, or whether I'm really hungry."

"Go ahead, eat," I said. "What else would you like?"

"Another meatball," she said, "a pickle and a glass of beer. You might as well take the glass." She emptied the glass and gave it to me. I went down into the bar, and while the woman behind the counter was filling the glass I had another schnapps. The woman looked at me more kindly than before, put a meatball and a pickle on a plate, and pushed it toward me across the wet counter. It was quite dark now outside. The bar was almost empty, and the people dancing in the lounge were noisy. After paying, I was left with only two marks.

"Will you be leaving early tomorrow?" the woman asked.

"Yes," I said.

"Then you'd better pay for the room now."

"I've already paid."

"Oh, I see," she said. "But please be sure to bring the glasses and plates down before you leave. We've learned the hard way. You will bring them down, won't you?"

"Of course," I said.

Käte was lying on her back, smoking.

"It's marvelous here," she said as I sat down beside

her, "a wonderful idea to go to a hotel again. It's a long time since we were in a hotel. Is it expensive?"

"Eight marks!"

"Do you still have that much?"

"I've already paid. All I've got now is two marks."

She took her purse, shook the contents out on the bed, and from among the toothbrush, soap container, lipstick, and medallions we fished out what was left of the money I had given her at the fairground. It was four marks.

"That's good," I said, "that's enough to go and have breakfast."

"I know a nice place," she said, "where we can have breakfast. Just beyond the underpass, on the left coming from here." I looked at her.

"It's very nice there, a charming girl and an old man. The coffee is good. That's where I made debts."

"Was the idiot boy there too?" I asked.

She took her cigarette from her lips and looked at me.

"Do you go there often?"

"No, I was there for the first time this morning. Shall we go there tomorrow morning?"

"Yes," she said. She rolled onto the other side toward the window and lay with her back to me. I wanted to pass her the plate and the beer, but she said: "Never mind, I'll eat it later."

I remained sitting beside her, although she had turned away, and sipped at my beer. It was quiet in the station. Through the window I could see, on the tall building beyond the station, the huge brandy bottle outlined in lights that always hangs there in the sky; in the hollow belly of the bottle one could see the silhouette of a man drinking. And at the top of the building the ever-changing messages: illuminated letters rolling out of the void. Slowly I read: USE YOUR HEAD—the line vanished —DON'T STAY IN BED—came tumbling out of the dark night—then nothing for a few seconds, and a curious tension filled me—WHEN YOU'RE HUNG OVER, there it was again, dropped back into the void, and again nothing for a few seconds, then suddenly all the letters lighting up at once: TAKE DOULORIN—three times, four times, it flared up red in front of the void: TAKE DOULORIN. Then in piercing yellow: YOU CAN TRUST YOUR DRUGGIST!

"Fred," Käte said suddenly, "I think if we discuss what you want to know, you haven't a hope. That's why I'd rather not discuss it. You must know what you have to do, but even if I am pregnant I don't want you to come home, to shout all over the place, strike the children although you know they're innocent. I don't want that. It wouldn't be long before we'd be shouting at each other. I don't want that. And I can't come to you any more either."

She was still lying with her back to me, and we both stared at the illuminated letters up there at the top of the tall building that were now changing, faster and faster, more and more abruptly, and in rainbow colors sending out into the night rainbow-hued words: YOU CAN TRUST YOUR DRUGGIST!

"Did you hear me?"

"Yes," I said, "I heard you. Why can't you come to me any more?"

"Because I'm not a prostitute. I've nothing against

154

prostitutes, Fred, but I'm not one of them. It's awful
for me to come to you, to lie with you somewhere in
the hallway of a ruined building or on a field, and then
ride home on the streetcar. I always have the awful
feeling that you've forgotten to slip five or ten marks
into my hand when I get on the streetcar. I don't know
what these women are paid when they've been with a
man."

"They get much less, I believe." I finished the beer,
turned toward the wall, looked at the heart-shaped
pattern of the green wallpaper. "I suppose that means
we'll separate."

"Yes," she said, "I think it's better. I have no inten-
tion of exerting any pressure on you, Fred—you know
me—but I think it's better for us to separate. The children no longer understand: they do believe me when I
say you're ill, but to them the word 'ill' means something different. Besides, all that yapping in the building's
affecting them. The children are growing up, Fred.
There are so many misunderstandings. Some people
even think you've got another woman. You haven't,
have you, Fred?" We were still lying back to back,
and it sounded as if she were speaking to a third person.

"No," I said, "I haven't got another woman, you
know that."

"One can never be sure," she said. "I've sometimes
had my doubts because I didn't know where you were
living."

"I haven't got another woman," I said, "I've never
lied to you, you know that."

She seemed to reflect. "No," she said, "I don't think

you've ever lied to me. Not that I can remember anyway."

"There you are then." I took a sip of her beer from the glass standing beside me on the chair.

"Come to think of it, you have a pretty easy life," she said. "You get drunk when you feel like it, you go for walks in cemeteries, you only have to phone me and I come when you desire me—and at night you sleep at this Dante scholar's."

"I don't sleep that often at the Blocks'. I usually find a spot somewhere else: I can't stand that house. It is so huge and empty and beautiful, so tasteful. I don't like these houses that are so tasteful."

I turned around, looked across her back at the illuminated sign up at the top of the building, but it was still the same: YOU CAN TRUST YOUR DRUGGIST!

All night long the words remained the same, flaring up over and over again in all the colors of the rainbow. We lay there for a long time, smoking and saying nothing. Later I got up and drew the curtains, but even through the thin curtains we could still see the words.

I was very surprised at Käte. She had never spoken to me like that. I let my hand rest on her shoulder and said nothing. She went on lying with her back to me, opened her purse, I heard the click of her lighter, and saw the smoke rising toward the ceiling from where she lay.

"Shall I turn out the light?" I asked.

"Yes, it's better."

I stood up, turned out the light, and lay down again beside her. She had turned onto her back, and I got a

shock when I groped for her shoulder and my hand
suddenly closed on her face; her face was wet with
tears. I couldn't find anything to say, I took my hand
away from there, searched under the cover for her
small firm hand and held it tight. I was glad she let me.

"Damn it all," she said in the dark, "every man ought
to know what he's doing when he gets married."

"I'll do all I can," I said, "really all I can to get us
an apartment."

"Don't be silly," she said, and it sounded as if she
were laughing. "It's got nothing to do with the apartment. Do you really think that's the problem?"

I raised myself, trying to look into her face. I let go
of her hand, saw her pale face below me, saw the narrow white street of her parting into which I had
dropped so often, and when the letters flared up again
at the top of the building I saw her face distinctly,
flooded in green: she really was smiling. I lay back
again, and now she sought my hand and held it tight.

"You really don't think that's the problem?"

"No," she said quite firmly, "no, no. Now be honest,
Fred. If I came to you and said I had found an apartment, would you be dismayed or would you be
pleased?

"I would be pleased," I said at once.

"You'd be pleased for our sake."

"No, I'd be pleased that I could come back to you all.
Oh, how can you even think. . . ."

It was quite dark now. We were lying back to back
again, and I turned now and then to see whether Käte
had turned around, but she stared at the window for

almost half an hour and said nothing, and when I turned I saw the words flare up high up at the top of the building: YOU CAN TRUST YOUR DRUGGIST!

From the station came the pleasant mumbling of the announcer, from the bar downstairs the noise of the people dancing, and Käte said nothing. I found it difficult to start speaking again, but I came out with: "Won't you at least have something to eat?"

"Yes," she said, "would you please pass me the plate and turn on the light."

I stood up, switched on the light, and lay down again with my back to her, heard her eating the pickle, the meatball. I also passed her the glass of beer, and she said "Thanks," and I heard her drink. I rolled onto my back and put my hand on her shoulder.

"It is really unbearable for me, Fred," she said softly, and I was glad that she was speaking again. "I understand you very well, maybe too well. I know the feelings you have, and know how marvelous it is to really wallow in filth, sometimes. I know that feeling—and it might be better if you had a wife who doesn't understand that at all. But you're forgetting the children—they're there, they're alive, and the way things are it's unbearable for me because of the children. You know what it was like when we both began drinking. It was you who begged me to stop."

"It was really terrible when we got home and the children could smell it. But it was my fault that you were drinking too."

"I'm not concerned with establishing who's guilty of what." She put down the plate and swallowed some beer. "I don't know, never will know, whether it was your fault or not, Fred. I don't want to offend you, Fred, but I envy you."

"You envy me?"

"Yes, I envy you, because you're not pregnant. You can even clear out, and I can even understand that. You go for walks, spend hours at the cemeteries, get drunk on your melancholy when you don't have the money for drink. You get drunk on your grief at not being with us. I know you love the children, and me too, you love us very much—but it never occurs to you that a condition you find so unbearable that you escape from it is slowly doing us to death, because you're not with us. And it never occurs to you that prayer is the only thing that might help. You never pray, do you?"

"Very rarely," I said. "I can't."

"Anyone can see that, Fred—you've grown old, you look really old, like a poor old bachelor. Sleeping now and again with your wife doesn't mean being married to her. During the war you once told me you would rather live in a filthy cellar with me than be a soldier. You weren't a youngster any more when you wrote that, you were thirty-six years old. Sometimes I do feel that the war put a kink in you. You used to be different."

I was very tired, and everything she was saying depressed me because I knew she was right. I wanted to ask her whether she still loved me, but I was afraid it might sound ridiculous. In the old days I was never afraid something might sound ridiculous, I used to tell her everything, just the way it occurred to me. But I did not ask her now whether she still loved me.

"Maybe," I said wearily, "the war did leave me with a scar. I'm almost always thinking about death, Käte, it's driving me crazy. In the war there were so many dead I never saw, only heard about. Indifferent voices read off numbers over the phone, and those numbers were the dead. I tried to imagine them, and I could imagine them: three hundred dead, that was a whole mountain. I once spent three weeks at what they called the front. I saw what the dead looked like. Sometimes I had to go out during the night to repair the line, and in the dark I often stumbled over the dead. It was so dark I couldn't see a thing, not a thing. Totally black, everything, and I crawled alongside the cable I was holding till I found the spot where it was ripped. I mended the wires, connected the testing set, crouching there in the dark, flung myself down when a flare rose up or a gun was fired, and spoke in the darkness with someone sitting thirty or forty yards away in a bunker —but it was far away, far away I tell you, farther than God can be away from us."

"God is not far away," she said softly.

"It was far away," I said, "many millions of miles away it was, the voice I was talking to to test whether the line was working again. Then I would crawl slowly back, holding the cable in my hand, stumble again in the darkness over the dead and sometimes stay lying beside them. Once it was the whole night. The others thought I was dead, they had looked for me and already given me up, but I lay all night beside the dead whom

I couldn't see, could only feel—I stayed beside them, I don't know why—and time didn't drag for me. When the others found me they thought I had been drunk. And I felt bored when I had to return to the living— you wouldn't believe how boring most people are, the dead are grand."

"You're terrible, Fred," she said, but she did not let go of my hand. "Give me a cigarette."

I fumbled for my cigarettes in my pocket, gave her one, struck a match, and leaned over her to see her face. She seemed to me to look younger, to be feeling better, her skin no longer so yellow.

"You don't feel sick any more?" I asked.

"No," she said, "not a bit. I'm fine. But I'm afraid of you, I really am."

"You needn't be afraid of me. It wasn't the war that did me in. It would be just the same—I'm simply bored. You should hear what goes into my ear all day long: most of it hot air."

"You should pray," she said, "you really should. It's the only thing that can never be boring."

"You pray for me," I said. "I used to be able to pray, I've lost the knack."

"It needs practice. You must persevere. Start over and over again. Drinking is no good."

"When I'm drunk, I can sometimes pray quite well."

"It's no good, Fred. Prayer is for the sober. It's like standing in front of one of those moving elevators and you're afraid to jump on, you have to keep bracing yourself, and suddenly you're in the elevator and it's carrying you up. Sometimes I can feel it quite distinctly, Fred, when I lie awake at night and cry, when at last everything is silent, then I often feel that I get through. Then I don't care about anything else, the room or the dirt, even the poverty, even your being away from us doesn't matter any more. After all, Fred, it's not for all that long, another thirty or forty years, and that's as long as we have to stick it out. And I feel we should try to stick it out together. Fred, you're kidding yourself, you're a dreamer, and dreaming is dangerous. I could understand it if you had left us for another woman. It would be terrible for me, much more than now, but I could understand it. If it were because of that girl, Fred, in the snack booth, I could understand it."

"Please," I said, "don't talk about it."

"But you went away to dream, that's not good. You like seeing her, don't you, the girl in the booth?"

"Yes, I like seeing her. I like seeing her very much. I shall often go and see her, but I would never dream of leaving you on her account. She is very devout."

"Devout? How do you know?"

"Because I saw her in church. I just saw her kneeling there and receiving the Blessing, I wasn't in the church more than three minutes, she was kneeling there with the idiot, and the priest blessed them both. But I saw how devout she is, saw it in her movements. I followed her because she touched my heart."

"What did she do?"

"She touched my heart."

"Did I also touch your heart?"

"You didn't touch my heart, you turned it upside

down. It made me quite ill at the time. I wasn't young any more," I said, "almost thirty, but you turned my heart upside down. That's what it's called, I believe. I love you very much."

"Have there been other women who touched your heart?"

"Yes," I said, "quite a few. There *were* a few who touched my heart. Actually I don't like putting it that way, but I don't know any better expression. Gently touched, is what I ought to say. Once in Berlin I saw a woman who touched my heart. I was standing at the window in the train, suddenly a train came in on the other side of the platform, a window stopped across from mine and the window was let down—it was all misted over—and I was looking into the face of a woman who immediately touched my heart. She was very dark and tall, and I smiled at her. Then my train started to move, I leaned out, waved, as long as I could see her. I never saw her again, never wanted to see her again."

"But she touched your heart. Tell me all these touching stories, Fred. Did she wave to you, too, that toucher of hearts?"

"Yes," I said. "She waved to me. I'd have to think a bit, I'm sure I'd remember the others. I have a good memory for faces."

"Come on now," she said, "think, Fred!"

"It often happens to me with children," I said, "with old men or old women too, for that matter."

"And I merely made your heart turn upside down."

"You touched it too," I said. "Oh my love, don't

force me to keep saying that word. When I think of you, it often happens: I see you coming down the stairs, strolling all by yourself through the city, I see you shopping, feeding the baby. Then it's like that for me with you."

"But that girl in the booth is very near."

"Maybe it'll be different when I see her again."

"Maybe," she said. "Do you want to finish my beer?"

"Yes," I said. She passed me her glass, and I drank it up. Then I got up, picked up the empty glasses and plates and took them downstairs. Two young men were standing at the counter, grinning at me as I put down the empty glasses and plates on the counter. Now the landlady with her white, poreless face was there again. She nodded to me. I immediately went upstairs again. Käte looked at me and smiled as I entered the room.

I switched off the light, undressed in the dark, and got into bed. "It's only ten o'clock," I said.

"Lovely," she said, "we can sleep for almost nine hours."

"How long is that young fellow staying with the children?"

"Till just before eight."

"But we don't want to hurry over breakfast," I said.

"Will someone wake us?"

"No, I'll wake up all right."

"I'm tired, Fred," she said, "but tell me some more. Don't you know any more touching stories?"

"Maybe I'll think of a few more," I said.

"Go ahead," she said. "You're a nice fellow, but there are times when I'd like to beat you up. I love you."

"I'm glad you said that. I was scared to ask you."

"We used to ask each other every three minutes."

"For years."

"For years," she said.

"Go ahead, tell me," she said, taking my hand again and clasping it.

"About women?" I asked.

"No," she said, "I'd rather hear about men or children, or about old women. I don't know whether I'm so sure about the young women."

"There's nothing for you to be afraid of," I said. I leaned over her, kissed her mouth, and when I lay back again my glance fell outside, and I saw the illuminated sign YOU CAN TRUST YOUR DRUGGIST!

"Go ahead," she said.

"In Italy," I said, "many people touched me. Men and women, young and old, children too. Even rich women. Rich men even."

"And a moment ago you said that people were boring."

"I feel quite different, much better, since I know you still love me. You've been saying some terrible things to me."

"I won't take back a word. Now we're playing a bit, Fred. Don't forget that we're playing. We'll be serious again soon enough. And I won't take back a word—and the fact that I love you doesn't mean a thing. You love the children too, but you couldn't care less how they get along."

"Oh, I know," I said. "You've made yourself quite clear. But now take your pick, whatever you like, man, woman, or child, and which country?"

"Holland," she said. "A Dutchman."

"Oh, that's mean," I said. "How do you expect me to find a Dutchman to touch your heart? You're mean, but during the war I really did once see a Dutchman who touched my heart, and a rich one at that. But he was no longer rich. As we were being driven through Rotterdam—it was the first ruined city I had seen; funny, now I've reached the point where a city that's not ruined depresses me—at the time I was all confused, I saw the people, saw the ruins. . . ."

I felt the grip on my hand loosening, leaned over her, and saw that she was asleep: in sleep her face looks arrogant, very detached, her lips are slightly parted with a look of suffering. I lay back again, smoked another cigarette, and lay awake in the dark for a long time, thinking about it all. I even tried to pray, but couldn't. For a moment I considered going downstairs again, perhaps to have at least one dance with a girl from the chocolate factory, to drink one more schnapps, and to play the machines a bit, they were bound to be free now. But I stayed where I was. Every time the slogan at the top of the building flared up, it illuminated the greenish wallpaper with the heart-shaped pattern, the shadow of the lamp appeared against the wall, and the pattern of the blankets: ball-playing bears that had turned into ball-playing men: bull-necked athletes tossing oversize soap bubbles at each other. But the last thing I saw before I fell asleep was the slogan up there:

YOU CAN TRUST YOUR DRUGGIST!

12

It was still dark when I woke up. I had slept deeply, and the moment I awoke I had a sense of great well-being. Fred was still asleep, turned toward the wall, I could see only his thin neck. I got up, drew aside the curtain, and saw above the station the pale gray of the dawn. Lighted trains were arriving, the subdued voice of the announcer wafted across the ruins to the hotel, the muffled rumbling of the trains could be heard. Everything was quiet in the building. I was hungry. I left the window open, got back into bed, and waited. But now I was restless, thought constantly of the children, longed for them, and had no idea what the time was. Since Fred was still asleep, it couldn't be six-thirty yet, he always wakes at six-thirty. I had plenty of time. I got up again, pulled on my coat, slipped into my shoes, and tiptoed around the bed. I cautiously opened the door, groped my way in the half-light through the dirty corridor toward the toilet, and finally found it in an unlit, smelly corner. Fred was still asleep when I got back. I could see the illuminated clocks in the station

—yellowish, glowing discs, but I couldn't read the time. At the top of the tall building the slogan flared up again, sharply etched in the gray darkness:

YOU CAN TRUST YOUR DRUGGIST!

I washed carefully, without making any noise, dressed, and when I looked around saw that Fred was watching me: he lay there blinking, lit a cigarette, and said: "Good morning."

"Good morning," I said.

"Don't you feel sick any more?"

"Not a bit," I replied. "I feel just fine."

"Good," he said, "no need to hurry."

"I have to leave, Fred," I said. "I'm getting anxious."

"Aren't we going to have breakfast together?"

"No," I said.

The chocolate-factory siren hooted loudly, its shrill whistle sliced three times into the morning. I sat on the edge of the bed, did up my shoelaces, and felt Fred thrust his hand into my hair from behind. He let it slip gently through his fingers and remarked: "If everything you said yesterday is true, I suppose it means we won't be seeing each other again for a while, so shouldn't we at least have a cup of coffee together?"

I said nothing, zipped up my skirt, buttoned my blouse, went over to the mirror, and combed my hair. I wasn't looking at myself in the mirror, but I combed my hair, and felt my heart beating. But now I realized everything I had said yesterday, and I didn't want to take it back. I had felt so absolutely sure that he would come back, but now everything seemed uncertain. I heard him get up, saw him in the mirror standing upright beside the bed, and it struck me how wretched he looked. He had slept in the shirt that he wore during the day, his hair was disheveled, he looked grumpy as he pulled on his trousers. I mechanically drew the comb through my hair. I had never seriously considered even the possibility that he might actually desert us, but now I did: my heart stood still, started racing, stopped again. I watched him closely as, cigarette in mouth, he listlessly buttoned his crumpled trousers, tightened his belt, pulled on his socks and shoes: there he stood, sighing, passing his hands over his forehead, his eyebrows, and I could not believe that I had been married to him for fifteen years: he was a stranger to me, that bored, listless person who now sat down on the edge of the bed, holding his head in his hands, and I let myself fall into the mirror and dwell on the vision of another life that would be without marriage: it must be marvelous, a life where there was no marriage, no bleary-eyed husbands who, barely awake, started groping for their cigarettes. I withdrew my eyes from the mirror, combed my hair into place, and went to the window. It was lighter now, pale gray above the station, I took it in without knowing: I was still dreaming of that life without marriage that has been promised us, hearing the rhythm of liturgical singing, saw myself in the company of men to whom I was not married, men I knew had no desire to penetrate my womb.

"May I use your toothbrush?" Fred asked from the washstand. I looked toward him, said hesitatingly, "Yes," and suddenly came to again.

"My God," I burst out, "you could at least take off your shirt while you're washing."

"Why should I?" he said. He tucked in the collar of his shirt, moistened a towel, wiped his face and neck, and the listlessness of his movements irritated me.

"I shall trust a druggist," he said, "and buy a trustworthy toothbrush. How about putting all our trust in the druggists?"

"Fred," I burst out again. "How can you make jokes! I've never seen you in such a good mood so early in the morning!"

"I'm not in a good mood at all," he said, "not even in a bad one, although it's hard to be cheerful without any breakfast, not even coffee."

"Oh, I know you," I said, "go and let your heart be touched."

He was using my comb, stopped now, turned around, and looked at me: "I invited you for breakfast, my love," he said gently, "and you haven't given me an answer yet."

He turned away again, went on combing his hair, and said into the mirror: "I won't be able to give you those ten marks till next week."

"Oh forget it," I said, "you don't have to give me all your money."

"But I would like to," he said, "and I ask you to accept it."

"Thank you, Fred," I said. "I appreciate that, I

really do. If we're going to have breakfast, we'd better hurry."

"So you're coming along?"

"Yes."

"Oh, good."

He pulled his tie through his collar, knotted it, and went over to the bed to pick up his jacket.

"I'll come back," he burst out, "come back for sure, come back to you, but I don't want to be forced into something I'd rather do on my own."

"Fred," I said, "I don't think there's anything more to discuss."

"No," he said, "you're right. It would be wonderful to see you again in a life in which I could love you as much as I do now without marrying you."

"I was just thinking about that," I whispered, and I could no longer hold back my tears.

He came quickly around the bed to me, put his arms around me, and I heard him say while his chin was resting on my head: "How wonderful it would be to see you there again. I hope you won't get a shock if I turn up there too."

"Oh, Fred," I said, "do think about the children."

"I am thinking about them," he replied. "I think about them every day. Won't you give me a kiss?"

I raised my head and kissed him.

He let go of me, helped me into my coat, and I packed our things in my bag while he finished dressing.

"The lucky ones," he said, "were those who did not love each other when they got married. It is terrible to love each other and to get married."

"Perhaps you're right," I said.

It was still dark, and in the corridor there was a smell from the corner where the toilet was. The restaurant downstairs was closed, there wasn't a soul in sight, not a door was open, and Fred hung the key on a big nail beside the entrance to the restaurant.

The street was filled with girls on their way to the chocolate factory: I was amazed to see how cheerful they looked, most of them were walking arm in arm and laughing together.

As we entered the snack booth, the cathedral bells struck a quarter to seven. The girl had her back to us, working the coffee machine. There was only one table free. The idiot sat crouched by the stove, sucking his lollipop. It was warm and smoky. The girl smiled at me as she turned around, said "Oh," then looked at Fred and again at me, smiled and hurried to the unoccupied table to wipe it off. Fred ordered coffee, rolls, and butter.

We sat down, and it did me good to see that she was really glad: her ears were slightly pink with exertion as she prepared our plates for us. But I was restless, kept on thinking about the children, and breakfast was not a success. Fred was restless too. I noticed that he rarely looked across to the girl, tried to look at me when my eyes were not on him, and whenever I did look at him he looked away. A lot of people came into the booth, the girl handed out rolls, sausage, and milk, counted out money, took some, and now and then she looked across at me and smiled, as if to confirm a private understanding. An understanding about something she seemed silently to take for granted. When things quieted down at bit she went over to the idiot, wiped his mouth, whispered his name in his ear. And I thought of everything she had told me about him. I was quite taken aback when suddenly the priest came in who had taken my confession yesterday. He smiled at the girl, gave her some money, and was handed a red pack of cigarettes across the counter. Fred was watching him intently too. Then the priest ripped open the pack, his gaze swept casually around the room, he saw me, and I saw him start. He was not smiling now, slipped the loose cigarette into the pocket of his black coat, started toward me, flushed, and stepped back again.

I got up and went toward him.

"Good morning, Father," I said.

"Good morning," he replied, looked around in embarrassment and whispered: "I must talk to you, I've already been to your home this morning."

"Why on earth?" I asked.

He took the cigarette from his coat pocket, put it between his lips, and whispered as he struck the match: "You are absolved, definitely—I was very stupid, forgive me."

"Thank you very much," I said. "How were things at home?"

"I only spoke to an elderly lady. Was that your mother?"

"My mother?" I asked horrified.

"Come and see me some time," he said, and left very quickly.

Fred said nothing when I returned to the table. He

looked very miserable. I put my hand on his arm. "I have to go, Fred," I said softly.

"Not yet, I must speak to you."

"Not here, later. My God, you had all night."

"I'm coming back," he whispered, "soon. Here's some money for the kids, I promised, didn't I? Buy them something, some ice cream maybe, if that's what they'd like."

He put down a mark. I took it and put it in my coat pocket.

"Later," he whispered, "you'll get what I owe you."

"Oh Fred," I said, "don't keep on."

"I must," he said. "It is so awful to think that we might. . . ."

"Phone me," I whispered back to him.

"You'll come if I phone?" he asked.

"Don't forget I still owe them for a coffee and three doughnuts."

"I won't. Do you really want to leave now?"

"I must."

He got up, I remained seated and watched him standing at the counter and waiting. The girl smiled across at me as Fred paid, and I got up and walked with Fred to the door.

"Come again!" she called, I called back: "I will!" and threw one more glance at the idiot, who was still sitting there crouched over his bare lollipop stick.

Fred took me to the bus stop. We didn't exchange a single word, gave each other a quick kiss when the bus arrived, and I saw him standing there as I have so often seen him: shabbily dressed and sad. I could just see him walking slowly off toward the station without once looking back.

I felt as if I had been away an eternity as I walked up the dirty stairs to our apartment, and I realized that I had never before left the children alone for so long. There was a subdued hubbub in the building, kettles were whistling, radios were dispensing their official good cheer, and on the second floor Mesewitz was bickering with his wife. Behind our apartment door there was not a sound: I pressed the bell three times, waited, and at last heard the children when Bellermann opened the door. I heard all three, greeted Bellermann hurriedly, and ran past him into the room to see the children: they were sitting around the table looking better behaved than they ever do with me. Their conversation, their laughter, ceased when I entered: there was only a moment's silence, and I felt a stab of anguish. I was afraid—for only a moment, but I'll never forget it, that moment.

Then the two older ones got up, hugged me, and I picked up the baby in my arms, kissed him, and felt the tears running down my face. Bellermann was already in his coat, holding his hat: "Did they behave well?" I asked.

"Yes," he said, "very well," and the children looked at him and smiled.

"Wait a moment," I said. I put the baby into his high chair, took my purse out of the drawer, and went out with Bellermann into the corridor. I saw Mrs. Franke's hat and Mr. Franke's cap lying on the hall table and said "Good morning" to Mrs. Hopf who was coming from the toilet. She had curlers in her hair and a magazine tucked under her arm. I waited till she was in her room, and looked at Bellermann and said:

"Fourteen, isn't it?"

"Fifteen," he said with a smile.

I gave him fifteen marks and said: "Thank you very much," and he replied: "It was a pleasure," then put his head once more around the door of our room and called out: "Good-bye, kids!" and the children called back: "Good-bye!"

I hugged them all once again when we were alone, gave them a searching look, and couldn't discover anything in their faces that would have justified my fears. With a sigh I began to make their sandwiches for school. Clemens and Carla were digging around in their boxes. Carla sleeps on an American army cot that we fold up during the day and hang from the ceiling, Clemens on an old plush sofa that he has long outgrown. Bellermann had even made the beds.

"Children," I said, "Father sends you his love. He has given me some money for you."

They said nothing.

Carla walked over to my side and picked up her sandwiches. I looked at her: she has Fred's dark hair, his eyes which can so suddenly take on a faraway look.

The baby was playing in his little chair, looking up at me from time to time as if he wanted to make sure I was still there, and went on playing.

"Have you both said your prayers?"

"Yes," said Carla.

"Father will soon be coming home," I said, and I felt a great tenderness for the children, had to make an effort not to start crying again.

Again the children said nothing. I looked at Carla, who was sitting beside me on a chair, leafing through a schoolbook and listlessly sipping her milk. And suddenly she looked up at me and said quietly: "He isn't sick at all, he's still giving lessons."

I turned around and looked at Clemens, who was sitting on the sofa bent over an atlas. He looked at me calmly and said:

"Beisem told me, he sits next to me."

I hadn't known that.

"There are some illnesses," I said, "where a person doesn't have to stay in bed."

The children said nothing. They went off with their school satchels, and I went out into the corridor and followed them with my eyes as they walked slowly along the gray street, their shoulders slightly hunched under the weight of the books, and I was overcome with sadness because I saw myself walking along a street, my satchel on my back, my shoulders slightly hunched under the weight of the books; I no longer saw the children, saw only myself, saw myself from above: a little girl with blond braids, thinking deeply about a knitting pattern or the date of Charlemagne's death.

When I came back, Mrs. Franke was standing in front of the hall mirror, twitching the mauve veil on her hat into place. The bells were ringing for eight-o'clock Mass. She said "Good morning," came toward me, confronted me with a smile in the dark corridor, blocking my way to our room.

"They say," she began in a friendly tone, "that your husband has finally left you. Is that right?"

"That's right," I said softly, "he has left me."

And I was amazed that I felt no more hatred.

"And he drinks, doesn't he?" And she knotted the veil around her pretty neck.

There was hardly a sound. From our room I could hear the gentle babble of my baby as he talked to his building blocks, I could hear the voice of the announcer, who said five times, six, seven times—I could hear it in the silence—"Seven thirty-nine—perhaps it's time to leave your charming wife, but perhaps you can still listen to Bulwer's cheery morning march...," I could hear the morning music, and that official good cheer fell upon me like the strokes of a lash. Mrs. Franke stood there in front of me, not moving, not speaking, but I saw the lethal brilliance of her eyes, yearned for the husky voice of the Negro that I had once heard, just once, and for which I have been waiting in vain ever since, the husky voice that sang:

"and never said a word."

And I said "Good-bye" to Mrs. Franke, pushed her aside, and went into my room. She said nothing. I picked up the baby, held him close, and heard Mrs. Franke going off to Mass.

13

The bus always stops at the same place. The bay where it has to stop is cramped, and every time it stops it gives a jolt that wakes me up. I stand up, get out, and after crossing the street I find myself in front of the window of a hardware store, looking at a sign: "Ladders—All Sizes—D.M. 3.20 per rung." It is pointless for me then to glance up at the clock on the building to make sure what time it is: it is exactly four minutes to eight—and if the clock says eight, or past eight, then I know the clock is fast: the bus keeps better time than the clock.

Every morning I stand for a few moments before the sign: "Ladders—All Sizes—D.M. 3.20 per rung." Next to the sign there is a three-runged ladder and, since summer began, next to the ladder a reclining chair with a life-size blonde woman made of papier-mâché or wax lying on it—I don't know what stuff they use for making mannequins—the woman is wearing sunglasses and reading a novel called *Vacation from Self*. I can't read the name of the author because it is hidden behind the beard of a plaster gnome leaning across an aquarium. There among coffee grinders, mangles, and the ladder lies the life-size blonde mannequin, and for the past three months she has been reading the novel *Vacation from Self.*

But today when I got out I saw that the sign, "Ladders—All Sizes—D.M. 3.20 per rung," was gone, and the woman who had spent the whole summer lying in the reclining chair reading *Vacation from Self* was now wearing a blue ski suit and standing on skis, her scarf blowing in the wind. Beside her was a sign: "Think Ahead to Winter Sports!"

I did not think ahead to winter sports, I turned into Melchior Street, bought five cigarettes at the kiosk to the left of the diocesan office, and walked past the doorman into the hallway. The doorman greeted me; he is one of my friends around here, will sometimes come and see me upstairs, smoke his pipe, and tell me the latest gossip.

I nodded to the doorman and greeted a few clerics who were hurrying up the stairs with their briefcases. Upstairs I opened the door to the switchboard room, hung up my coat and beret, tossed my cigarettes onto the table, followed by my loose change, plugged in the contact, and sat down.

Calm settles over me when I am seated at my workplace: I have the soft humming in my ear, say "Exchange" when someone in the building has dialed twice, when the red light goes on, and make the connection. I counted my money lying on the table—it was one mark twenty—rang the doorman, said "Bogner speaking, good morning," when he answered.

"Has the newspaper come yet?"

"Not yet," he said. "I'll bring it up when it does."

"Anything special happen?"

"Nothing."

"See you later then."

"See you later."

At eight-thirty came the personnel report which Bresgen, the office manager, phones in every day to Monsignor Zimmer. Everyone is scared stiff of Zimmer, even the priests working in the building who have been transferred from pastoral duties to the administration. He never says "Please," never says "Thank you," and my flesh creeps each time he dials and I answer. Every morning he says it at eight-thirty sharp:

"Monsignor Zimmer."

I heard Bresgen reporting: "Off sick: Weldrich, Zick, Chaplain Huchel. Not yet excused: Chaplain Soden."

"What's the matter with Soden?"

"No idea, sir."

I heard a sigh from Zimmer, as I often do when Soden's name is spoken, and that was the end of the first conversation.

It is close to nine before the daily orgy of telephoning gets underway. Incoming calls, outgoing calls, longdistance calls that I have to put through; now and again I get on the line, listen to the conversation, and come to the conclusion that here too the vocabulary hardly exceeds a hundred and fifty words. The most commonly used word is *careful*. It crops up over and over again, shows up in the general verbiage.

"The Leftist press has attacked H.E.'s speech. Careful."

"The Rightist press has ignored H.E.'s speech. Careful."

"The Christian press has praised H.E.'s speech. Careful."

"Soden's away without an excuse. Careful."

"Bolz has an audience at eleven. Careful."

H.E. is the abbreviation for His Eminence the Bishop. The divorce adjudicators speak Latin even on the phone when they are conversing professionally: I always listen in although I don't understand a word. Their voices are solemn, though it's odd to hear them laughing at Latin jokes. Strange that those two men, Father Pütz and Monsignor Serge, are the only ones around here who show a liking for me. At eleven Zimmer called the Bishop's confidential secretary: "I suggest a protest against the vulgarity of the druggists— but be careful. Desecration if not mockery of the Hieronymus Procession. Careful." Five minutes later the Bishop's secretary-general called back: "His Eminence will launch the protest at a private level. A cousin of His Eminence is President of the Druggists' Federation. Be careful."

"What was the result of the audience with Bolz?"

"Nothing definite yet, but I repeat: be careful."

Shortly after that, Monsignor Zimmer asked to be put through to Monsignor Weiner:

"Six transfers from the neighboring diocese."

'What are they like?"

"Two are straight E's, three are C minus, one of them seems to be good. Huckmann. Old-established family."

"I know them, first-rate family. What was it like yesterday?"

"Appalling, the battle continues."

"What's that?"

"Continues, the battle—there was vinegar in the salad."

"And yet you had. . . ."

". . . expressly insisted for months on lemon. Can't take vinegar. Open defiance."

"Who do you think's behind it?"

"W.," said Zimmer. "I'm sure it's W. I feel terrible."

"Dreadful business, we'll get back to it later."

"Yes, later."

So I was very nearly let in on a battle that was apparently being fought with drops of vinegar.

Around eleven-fifteen Serge phoned me.

"Bogner," he said, "how would you like to go into town?"

"I can't get away, sir."

"I'll have someone relieve you, for half an hour. Just to the bank. If you feel like it. There are times when one likes to get away."

"Who's going to relieve me?"

"Miss Hanke. My secretary isn't here, and Miss Hanke can't go because of her hip. How about it?"

"Fine," I said.

"That's what I thought. Come up as soon as Miss Hanke gets there."

Miss Hanke came right away. I always get a bit of a shock when she comes into my room with that strange rocking movement of her body. She always relieves me when I have to go out: to go to the dentist or run errands for Serge because he wants me to have a change. Miss Hanke is tall, lean, and dark, her hip trouble started only three years ago, when she was twenty, and I never tire of looking at her face: it is delicate, marked by gentleness. She brought me some flowers, mauve asters, and put them in the pot by the window before shaking hands with me.

"Run along," she said. "How are the kids?"

"Fine," I said, "they're fine." I put on my coat.

"Bogner," she said with a smile, "someone saw you drunk. Just so you know, in case Zimmer brings it up."

"Thank you," I said.

"You shouldn't drink."

"I know."

"And your wife," she asked cautiously, "how is your wife?"

I buttoned up my coat, looked at her, and said: "Tell me everything. What are they saying about my wife?"

"They're saying she's expecting again."

"Damn it," I said, "my wife's only known since yesterday."

"The grapevine knew it before your wife did."

"Miss Hanke," I said, "what's going on?"

She took a call, made the connection, looked at me with a smile: "Nothing special, really not: they say that you drink, that your wife is pregnant—besides, you've been separated from your wife for quite a while."

"Of course."

"Well, there you are. I can only warn you, of Zimmer, of Bresgen, of Miss Hecht, but you also have friends around here, more friends than enemies."

"I don't believe it."

"It's true," she said, "particularly among the clerics, almost all of them like you"—she smiled again—"birds of a feather, you know—and you're not the only one who drinks."

I laughed. "Tell me one more thing: who is having Zimmer slowly murdered with drops of vinegar?"

"You don't know?" she laughed at me in surprise.

"I really don't."

"Good God, half the diocese is laughing about it, and you of all people don't know, and you're sitting at the center of all the gossip! All right: It's Wupp—Deacon Wupp has a sister who's in charge of the kitchen at the Convent of the Blue Mantle of the Virgin. Need I say more?"

"Go on," I said. "I haven't a clue."

"Zimmer kept Wupp from becoming a prelate. Countermove: fifty pfennigs for a bottle of the cheapest vinegar, which is brought out from some hidden corner of the kitchen at the Convent of the Blue Mantle of the Virgin the moment Zimmer appears for a meal. But now run along, Serge is waiting for you."

I gave her a nod and left. Whenever I have talked to Miss Hanke, I am filled with a strange lightness, she has the gift of making things seem weightless, with her even the most piercing gossip turns into a harmless parlor game in which you are expected to join.

In the whitewashed corridor leading to Serge's office, baroque sculptures are cemented into the walls. Serge was sitting at his desk, head in hand. He is still a young man, some years younger than I am, and he is considered an authority on marital law.

"Good morning, Mr. Bogner," he said. I said: "Good morning," walked toward him, and he shook hands with me. He has the extraordinary gift, when I see him the day after borrowing money from him, of making me feel that he has forgotten about the money. Perhaps he really does forget about it. His office is one of the few that was not destroyed: the showpiece is a baroque tiled stove in the corner which, the catalogue of artistic monuments points out, was never lit because the prince-elector spent the winters in a smaller palace. Serge handed me a few checks and an envelope containing cash.

"There's sixty-two marks there," he said, "and eighty pfennigs. Please deposit the checks and the cash to our account. You know the number?"

"I do."

"I'm glad to get rid of it," he said. "Fortunately Witsch is returning the day after tomorrow and I can hand all this stuff back to him."

He gazed at me with his large, calm eyes, and I felt he was expecting me to start talking about my marriage. It's true he could probably give me some advice; on the other hand I am for him, of course, a case with an interesting background. In his face I see kindness and intelligence, I would like to speak to him, but I can't bring myself to. Sometimes I think I would talk to a slovenly priest, would even confess to him, I also know that nobody's to blame for being clean, for loving cleanliness, and Serge, of whose kindness I am aware, is the last person I would blame for it, yet the immaculate whiteness of his collar, the precise way the mauve border shows beyond the edge of his cassock, discourage me from speaking to him.

I put the money and the checks into the inner pocket of my coat, glanced up again, and found myself still looking into those large, calm eyes that never seemed to leave my face. I could sense that he wanted to help me, that he knew everything, whereas *I* knew that he would never bring up the subject. I returned his gaze until he slowly began to smile, and I suddenly asked him a question I had been wanting to ask a priest for many years:

"Do you believe, sir, that the dead rise again?"

I watched his handsome, clean face narrowly, keeping my eyes firmly on it; it did not change, and he said quietly:

"Yes."

"And do you believe," I went on—but he interrupted me, raised his hand, and said quietly: "I believe everything, everything you want to ask me. Otherwise I would immediately take off this gown, would become a divorce attorney, leave this whole pile behind me," he pointed to a big stack of files on his desk, "I would burn it because it would then be meaningless to me, as well as meaningless to those who torment themselves because they believe the same thing."

"Forgive me," I said.

"Oh, for what?" he said softly. "I believe you have a better right to ask me than I would to ask you."

"Don't ask me," I said.

"I won't," he said, "but one day you will speak, won't you?"

"Yes," I said, "one day I'll speak."

I picked up the newspaper from the doorman, counted my money once again outside the entrance, and walked slowly into town. I thought of many things: of the children, of Käte, of what Serge and what Miss Hanke had told me. All of them were right, and I was wrong, but none of them knew, not even Käte, how much I really longed for my children, for Käte too, and there were moments when I believed that I was right and all the others were wrong because they all could express themselves so well, and I could never find the words.

I wondered whether I should buy myself a cup of coffee and read the paper, the street noises sounded muffled although I was walking right through them. Someone was hawking bananas.

I stopped in front of Bonneberg's windows, looked at the fall overcoats, at the faces of the mannequins that always frighten me. I counted the checks in the inside pocket of my coat, made sure the envelope with the cash was still there, and suddenly my glance fell into the arcade dividing Bonneberg's windows: I saw a woman, and the sight of her touched my heart and at the same time aroused me. The woman was no longer young, but she was beautiful, I saw her legs, the green skirt, the shabbiness of her brown jacket, saw her green hat, but above all I saw her gentle, sad profile, and for a moment—I don't know for how long—my heart stopped; I saw her through two panes of glass, saw that she was looking at the clothes but at the same time thinking of something else—I felt my heart beating again, still saw the profile of that woman, and suddenly I knew it was Käte. Once again she seemed a stranger to me, for a few seconds I was assailed with doubt, I felt hot all over, and I thought I was going mad, but now she walked on, I followed her slowly, and when I saw her without the panes of glass I knew it really was Käte.

It was Käte, but she was different, quite different from the way I remembered her. Still she seemed to me, as I followed her along the street, to be at the same time a stranger and very familiar, my wife with whom I had spent the whole night, to whom I had been married for fifteen years.

"Maybe I'm really going mad," I thought.

I was startled when Käte went into a store, I stopped beside a vegetable cart, watched the entrance to the store, and far behind me, as if he were calling up to me from some nether region, I heard the man standing right next to me: "Cauliflowers, cauliflowers! Two for a mark!"

Although it was absurd, I was afraid Käte would never come out of the store again: I watched the entrance, looked into the grinning face of a cardboard

Javanese holding a cup of coffee up to his shiny teeth, heard the voice of the vegetable hawker as if from a deep cave: "Cauliflowers, cauliflowers! Two for a mark!" and I thought of very many things, didn't know what, and was startled to see Käte suddenly emerging from the store. She walked along Grüne Street, walked very fast, and I panicked whenever I lost sight of her for a few seconds, but then she stopped in front of a toy shop window, and I could observe her, her sad profile, I saw her figure that had lain beside me at night for so many years, that I had seen only four hours ago and that now I had not recognized.

When she turned around I quickly stepped behind the stand of a huckster, I could observe her without her seeing me. She looked into her shopping bag, pulled out a piece of paper, studied it, and beside me the man was shouting:

"If you stop to think, gentlemen, that you shave for fifty—yes, fifty years, so that your skin...."

But Käte walked on, and I didn't hear the end of the huckster's speech, I followed my wife, and at forty paces behind her crossed the streetcar tracks that converge at Bildoner Square. Käte stopped at a flower stall, I saw her hands, saw her quite clearly, her to whom I was more closely bound than to any other human being on earth: with whom I had not only slept, eaten, talked, for ten continuous years—there was something that bound me to her more than sleeping together: there had been a time when we had prayed together.

She bought some big yellow marguerites, some white

ones too, then went on, slowly, very slowly, she who had just been walking so fast, and I knew what she was thinking about. She always says: I buy the flowers that grow in the meadows where our children have never played.

So we walked along, one behind the other, both thinking of the children, and I didn't have the courage to catch up and speak to her. I hardly heard the sounds surrounding me: very far away, very faintly, the voice of an announcer droned in my ear as he shouted into the microphone: "Attention, please! Special streetcar service on Line H to the Druggists' Exhibition—Attention, please! Special streetcar service on Line H...."

I swam after Käte as if through gray water, could no longer count my heartbeats, and again I was startled when Käte entered the convent church, and the black, leather-padded door closed behind her.

It was only then that I noticed that the cigarette I had lighted when passing the doorman on my way out of the diocesan office was still burning: I threw it away, opened the church door, heard the sound of organ modulations, walked back across the square, sat down on a bench, and waited.

I waited for a long time, trying to imagine what it had been like in the morning when Käte got on the bus, but I couldn't imagine anything—I felt lost, lethargically floating along on an endless current, and the only thing I could see was the black church door from which Käte had to emerge.

When she actually did come, I didn't realize it was

she: she was walking faster, had placed the big, long-stemmed flowers between the handles of her bag, and I had to hurry to keep up with her as she swiftly walked across Bildoner Square back into Grüne Street: the flowers bounced to the rhythm of her steps, I felt sweat in my palms, staggered a bit, while my heart was filled with an aching throb.

She stopped in front of Bonneberg's window, I just had time to slip into the arcade and now saw her standing where I had just been standing, saw her gentle, sad profile, watched her size up the fall overcoats for men, and whenever Bonneberg's heavy swing door opened I heard the loudspeaker from inside:

"Coats? At Bonneberg's! Hats? At Bonneberg's! Suits? At Bonneberg's! For hat or jacket, coat or tie, Bonneberg's is your best buy!" Käte turned away, crossed the street, stopped at a soft-drink stand, and once again I saw her small hands pushing money across the counter, picking up change, putting it in her purse, tiny movements that I knew, that now caused a great pain in my heart. She poured lemonade into a glass, drank, and from inside the voice shouted:

"Coats? At Bonneberg's! Hats? At Bonneberg's! Suits? At Bonneberg's! For hat or jacket, coat or tie, Bonneberg's is your best buy!"

She slowly pushed back the bottle, the glass, picked up the flowers with her right hand, and once again I saw her leave, my wife, whom I had embraced in-numerable times without recognizing her. She walked quickly, seemed restless, kept on looking back, and I would duck, bend down, feel pain when her hat was swallowed up for an instant, and when she came to a halt at the Number 12 streetcar stop on Gersten Street, I escaped into a little tavern across from the streetcar stop.

"A schnapps," I said to the round, red face of the owner.

"A large one?"

"Yes," I said, and I saw the Number 12 arriving outside and Käte getting on.

"Here you are, sir," said the owner.

"Thanks," I said, and gulped down the large schnapps.

"Care for another one?" The owner gave me a long look.

"No, thanks," I said. "How much?"

"Eighty pfennigs."

I put down a mark, and slowly, still keeping his eyes on me, he counted out twenty pfennigs into my hand, and I left.

Along Gersten Street, across Moltke Square, I slowly retraced my steps to the diocesan office, without knowing what I was doing; past the doorman into the white-washed corridor, past the baroque sculptures, knocked on Serge's door and went in when no one answered.

For a long time I sat at Serge's desk, looked at the stack of files, heard the phone ring, let it ring. I heard laughter from the corridor—again the phone rang, loudly, but I only came to when Serge said behind me:

"Well, Bogner, back so soon?"

"Soon?" I said without turning around.

"Yes," he laughed, "hardly twenty minutes," but then he stood in front of me and looked at me, and I could see from his face what had happened: I saw it all, was suddenly wide awake, and I could tell from his face that his first thought was for the money. He thought something had happened to the money. I saw it in his face.

"Bogner," he said softly, "are you ill, or drunk?"

I drew the checks out of my pocket, the envelope with the cash, and held it all out to Serge: he took it and, without looking at it, put it down on his desk.

"Bogner," he said. "Tell me what happened."

"Nothing," I said. "Nothing's happened."

"Do you feel ill?"

"No," I said. "I'm thinking about something, I've just remembered something," and I saw it all again behind Serge's clean face, saw Käte, my wife, heard someone shout: "Coats?" saw Käte again, the whole length of Grüne Street, I saw the shabbiness of her brown jacket, heard someone announcing a special streetcar service on Line H to the Druggists' Exhibition, saw the black church door, saw long-stemmed yellow marguerites intended for the graves of my children, someone shouted: "Cauliflowers!"—I saw, heard, everything again, saw Käte's sad, gentle profile through Serge's face.

When he turned away I saw on the white wall above the tiled stove that had never been lit: a cardboard Javanese holding a cup of coffee up to his shiny white teeth.

194

"A car," Serge was saying into the phone, "send a car immediately."

Then I saw his face again, felt money in my hand, and looked down at it: a shining five-mark piece, and Serge said: "You must go home."

"Yes," I said. "Home."

ABOUT THE AUTHOR

Heinrich Böll, winner of the Nobel Prize for literature in 1972, is one of the most prolific, and most popular, of postwar German writers. Since 1947 he has been widely acclaimed for his novels and short stories, which have focused principally on the Second World War, its aftermath, and the havoc it wreaked on the people of Germany; his fiction constitutes a "working-through," not merely a remembering, of this horrendous Nazi experience. A master storyteller, Mr. Böll is in the first rank of contemporary European writers. Among his many books previously published in this country are: *Billiards at Half-past Nine* (1962); *The Clown* (1965); *End of a Mission* (1968); *Group Portrait with Lady* (1973); *The Lost Honor of Katharina Blum* (1975); *The Bread of Those Early Years* (1976); and *Missing Persons and Other Essays* (1977).

Heinrich Böll is a past President of the International P.E.N. and in that capacity has been active on behalf of writers throughout the world. He and his wife live in Cologne but spend much of their time at their farmhouse in a tiny hamlet in the foothills of the Eifel range.

Catalog

If you are interested in a list of fine Paperback
books, covering a wide range of subjects
and interests, send your name and address,
requesting your free catalog, to:

McGraw-Hill Paperbacks
1221 Avenue of Americas
New York, N.Y. 10020